Close Kin

BOOK II ★ THE HOLLOW KINGDOM TRILOGY

CLARE B. DUNKLE

Close Kin

Henry Holt and Company
New York

Special thanks to my editor, Reka Simonsen,
for her prompt, good-humored guidance and her strong
commitment to bringing out the best in her authors.

Henry Holt and Company, LLC
Publishers since 1866
115 West 18th Street
New York, New York 10011
www.henryholt.com

Henry Holt is a registered trademark of Henry Holt and Company, LLC
Copyright © 2004 by Clare B. Dunkle
All rights reserved.
Distributed in Canada by H. B. Fenn and Company Ltd.

Library of Congress Cataloging-in-Publication Data
Dunkle, Clare B.
Close kin / Clare B. Dunkle.—1st ed.
p.   cm.
Sequel to: The hollow kingdom.
Summary: After the mostly human Emily rejects the elvish Seylin's marriage
proposal, both undertake separate quests to learn about their true natures and
discover a royal elf and orphaned goblin to bring to the goblin kingdom.
ISBN 0-8050-7497-X
EAN 978-0-8050-7497-0
[1. Goblins—Fiction. 2. Elves—Fiction. 3. Magic—Fiction.
4. Marriage—Fiction.] I. Title.
PZ7.D92115C1 2004
[Fic]—dc22   2003057048

First Edition—2004
Book designed by Donna Mark
Printed in the United States of America on acid-free paper. ∞

1 3 5 7 9 10 8 6 4 2

For my daughters, Valerie and Elena,
who read it when they were homesick,
and for Kristyne, who loves Sable best

Close Kin

Prologue

Sable sat beside the dead body of her best friend, too miserable to cry. Only seventeen years old, she had already seen three elf women die in childbirth. She and Laurel had grown up together, and she couldn't comprehend yet that Laurel had left her to face life alone. Instead, another thought held her attention with cold finality. Sable was now the oldest girl in the camp. She would be the next to die.

As the weeks passed, Sable struggled with her grief. Laurel's death had left a gap that was almost like a visible thing: a blur where she should have sat with her weaving, or a blank where she always swam and splashed in the lake. Life was fragile. Sable had always known this. But did it have to be so predictable? She felt the pain of her loss turn into a new determination. Little by little, she made her plans.

The full moon came again, magnificent in its pale perfection. Sable sat on a hill above the camp, watching it rise over the lake. An elf man came to sit beside her.

"I looked everywhere for you," he said. She didn't reply. He looked at that flawless face, those dark blue eyes, that long hair that was blacker than the night. She was the most beautiful thing he knew.

"It's your marriage moon," he said softly, thinking about how long he had waited to see it. She was a woman now. She was eighteen.

"It's not my marriage moon," she answered. "It's just the moon. I told you I won't marry you, Thorn."

The man gave a grimace of annoyance. He had hoped that, once she wasn't a child any longer, she'd stop this childish talk, but he had already been expecting trouble. Sable should have been at the evening meal to renew the vows they had made years ago at their engagement. Then he would have given Sable her food, as he always did, and that simple ceremony would have made her his wife. But when he had woken up in the twilight, she was already gone. The band had eaten its meal without her.

"I've hunted your food since you were twelve," he pointed out. "I've sheltered and fed you since before your father died. I've been good to you, Sable. You know that I love you."

Sable looked at the man then, at his bright blond hair and gray eyes, his broad cheekbones, firm mouth, and strong chin. She had always idolized him, just as Laurel had idolized Rowan. "I'm not going to die like that, Thorn," she said. "If you loved me, you wouldn't want me to."

Thorn studied her, puzzled and impatient. She'd been so moody these last few weeks.

"Of course I don't want you to die," he protested. "But I don't make the rules. It's just life. If women don't die, there won't be any children."

"Laurel died, and there wasn't a child anyway," whispered Sable.

"That happens sometimes," said Thorn with a shrug, "and we all miss her, but she and Rowan were happy for a whole year and a half. And she wasn't sorry, either. She knew that's a woman's life." He put an arm around Sable, stroking that glossy black hair. "We'll have a happy year, too. I promise." He bent his head to kiss her. Sable had waited years for that kiss, but she pulled away.

"No," she said steadily. "I won't marry you."

Thorn was angry now. Nature hadn't blessed him with a very large store of patience, and it was rapidly running out.

"We're getting married," he said. "I don't care how silly you're going to be about it. Your father would have beaten you for this kind of talk; you know how much he wanted you to have a child."

"My father killed two wives to have me, just so his own name could pass on!" cried Sable. "I'm not going to die like that, Thorn! I'm not!"

"Sable," growled Thorn, taking her face between his hands, "who gave you every single meal you've eaten for the last six years?"

"You did," she whispered unhappily.

"And whose tent did you wake up in this evening?"

"Yours," she said again.

"Are you going to hunt your own food from now on?"

No answer. Sable wouldn't look at him. He looked at her instead, at that beautiful face, that perfect white skin, and he remembered again how much he loved her.

"No, you're not," he concluded. "Because you're going to be my wife, and I'll be your husband, and I hunt for you. And it's our marriage moon at last, and that's how it's going to be."

Sable glanced up, her blue eyes grave, to study the man who loved her. The man who wanted to kill her. She stared at him for a long moment, calm with despair.

"Then I need some time to get ready," she murmured and hurried back to the tents to gather the things she would need. Four cloths should be enough, and she retrieved the treasured triangle of broken glass that once, long before her birth, had been part of a hand mirror.

Sable propped the fragment of mirror carefully in the corner of the tent and took her father's hunting knife from under her sleeping pallet. She looked at the bone-white color of the true elf blade that never lost its edge, the way their metal knives did. She started to cry, thinking about what she must do, staring at her face in the shard of glass as if she were trying to memorize it. It was the last time, she decided. She would never look at it again.

Watching in the glass, she made the first cut, and the good elf blade hardly hurt her, it was so sharp. She made that whole cut before the smarting came. The blood covered up her cheek so that she couldn't see what she was doing, but she finished the two parallel cuts and then paused, a little dizzy. Should she go on to the other side before she did the really hard part? What if she fainted before she was done?

"Sable?" Irina was at the tent opening. "Thorn says you're going to repeat your vows soon. Are you getting ready? Can I help?"

Sable quickly put down the knife and turned her uninjured cheek toward the child.

"No," she gasped, Irina's face dim before her eyes, and the cloth in her hand warm and wet. "Wait. . . . Yes, you can, dear. Go and gather me some flowers."

"What kinds? What colors?" asked Irina happily, pleased to be of use.

"Oh, anything," Sable roused herself to answer. "Something pretty." And the child was gone.

Hands shaking, she made the twin cuts across the other cheek, watching in the glass to make them even. That's stupid, she told herself. Why would it matter? But it gave her something to think about besides the sting of the blade. Blood was running down her neck. It made her hands sticky and slippery, and it was hard to hold the knife.

Now for the hard part, and then I'll be done. She paused for a second and blinked until the mirror swam back into focus. Like butchering deer, she told herself firmly. Like flaying hide. And she sawed the sharp knife between the two cuts on her right cheek, peeling away the skin.

Blood was everywhere. She couldn't remember what she was doing. She couldn't quite understand why all this had to happen. "Butchering deer," she whispered, and gave a sob as the skinned cheek blazed with pain. Automatically, she turned the knife to the stretch of skin on the other cheek. Almost finished now.

"Do you want more of these?" It was Irina again.

Sable dropped the knife and stared at the blood running onto her dress, at her red hands holding the pieces of bloody skin. The red knife, the red hands began to turn gray before her eyes. I need air, she thought. I can't breathe. She crawled toward the tent opening.

Irina screamed and dropped the flowers as she scrambled away. Crawling from the tent, Sable heard shouts and running feet. Something must be wrong, she thought. I wonder what it is. She saw Rowan run up and then stop, pale and staring. She heard Thorn call her name and felt him grab her by the arms.

"Sable, what did you do?" he yelled frantically. As the world spun, she saw his handsome face for a second, twisted in horror and disgust. "Oh, Sable, no! You've —you've made yourself *ugly!*"

Ugly, thought the bloody girl. Yes, that was what was wrong. She was ugly, and she would never be beautiful again. But she was safe. She wouldn't die. He wouldn't marry her now. She slumped unconscious in the arms of the man who had loved her and wanted to kill her.

Chapter One

Seylin hurried through the maze of hallways in the great underground goblin palace and knocked on Emily's door. They had been close friends since childhood, but Seylin wasn't a child anymore. He was one of the King's Guard now, and his black uniform matched his black hair and eyes. The girl he had played with had grown into a young woman. By human standards, Emily looked quite average, and the elvish Seylin looked quite remarkable, but Seylin was the one who found himself daydreaming about Emily's brown eyes and warm smile. He couldn't even tell if she cared about him.

There was a scramble, and Emily's door popped open to reveal his friend Brindle's little daughter, her snake eyes gleaming up at him. In her arms she clutched Talah, Emily's monkey, rolled up in a blanket like a doll.

"Where's Em?" he asked, and the little girl pointed wordlessly behind her. He found Emily seated on the terrace, teaching a very small goblin boy to fasten a buckle. Emily was always surrounded by children. They appealed to her high spirits and love of excitement. Goblin babies were more fun than human babies, she said, because human babies never bit large chunks out of the furniture or tried to take off on awkward wings and crashed into the wall.

The handsome Seylin was an embarrassing anomaly in an ugly goblin world. His parents had almost died of shame over their son's striking features. Having grown up with teasing, inaudible whispers, and sympathetic glances, the sensitive young man had always enjoyed the company of Emily's many visiting children because he never felt that they were mocking him or gossiping over his looks. But, lately, he had found all the bustle and confusion a little hard to take.

"Can't I ever see you alone?" he asked crossly, sitting down beside her.

"Goodness, I am alone," responded the young woman. "Just Brindle's two before class this morning. This afternoon I'm expecting a dozen. We're going to the kitchens to bake cakes."

Seylin sighed. She was right. This was as alone as she ever was.

"Em, I've been thinking," he began. "We're older now, and I wanted to talk to you. After all, we're not little pages anymore." He paused. "We need to talk."

"I've been wanting to talk to you, too," declared Emily with some force. "Ever since you came back from that trading journey last spring, all you do is stand around and goggle at me. You hardly say five words, and if I look like I'm having any fun, you glower at me just like an old governess."

Seylin was glowering now. He tried to make himself stop. "That's not what I want to talk about," he protested. "What I wanted to say is that I won't always be a guard—"

"Nothing wrong with the Guard," remarked Emily breezily. "Thaydar told me last night he thinks the Guard's never looked better. Sweetie, we'd better run you to the potty," she added, standing up with the tiny goblin.

"So Thaydar was here again!" snapped Seylin.

"Not now," called Emily, hurrying off and leaving him free to glower unobserved. Thaydar, the cat-eyed commander of the Guard, was his most serious rival for Emily's affection. Thaydar made no secret of the fact that he wanted the prestige of a nongoblin bride, and he was one of the most important men in the kingdom.

To make matters worse, he was Seylin's commanding officer. Seylin had spent many evenings on patrol duty knowing that Thaydar was keeping Emily company back home.

After a few minutes of gloomy contemplation, Seylin wandered back into the apartment to find Emily breaking up a fight between the two children. Each of them had one of Talah's arms and refused to let go.

"No monkey for either of you," said Emily, prying them loose. Talah bounced into Seylin's arms, and he sat down on the couch with her.

"Em, I don't want to be a guard all my life," he continued earnestly. "There's nothing to guard. It's so boring. I don't want to be a lore-master, either, teaching the Unlock Spell over and over to crowds of pages, and I don't want to be a scholar. They just study things. I want to live stories, not read them."

Emily was pouring drinks and barely paying attention. She had heard all of this before. The little boy promptly dumped his cup down his front. She carried him over to the couch and sat down, scrubbing him off with a towel.

"Did I tell you that Jacoby was here last night," she said, "and he choked on a piece of caramel? I had to whack him on the back for a long time before it went down. I've learned something, Seylin. Goblins with beaks shouldn't eat chewy candy. They don't have any way to chew it."

"Why do I ever try to talk to you?" cried Seylin. "You never listen to a word I say!"

"I'm listening," she protested. "You don't want to be anything."

"Right," he confirmed, trying to ignore the fact that the little girl was staring at him fixedly with her hypnotic snake eyes. "Right, I won't always be a guard, I promise. I'll be something more. I know I don't have much to offer you right now," he continued as the little girl dragged Talah from his arms. "But I think I will later."

"Thanks, I don't need anything," answered Emily absently. "Did you see Jacoby's new sister? Isn't she adorable, with those little pink bird-feet?" Seylin gritted his teeth, glaring at his heedless beloved. Here he was, sitting right next to her, and she might as well be a thousand miles away.

"Kitty, kitty," giggled Brindle's daughter, patting his knee.

"Very good! Kitty," said Emily encouragingly. "Seylin, change into a cat for her."

"Em, I am trying to have an important conversation!" shouted Seylin. "I will not change into a cat!"

Brindle's daughter drew back and buried her face in Emily's lap.

"And I suppose it's more important than making a little child happy," said Emily angrily, stroking the girl's hair as she cried.

"Yes! Yes, as a matter of fact, it is," declared Seylin, breathing hard.

"Well, go have it somewhere else, then," ordered the righteous young woman. "I don't want to hear it."

"No, you don't, do you?" exclaimed Seylin, beside himself. "But you want to hear Thaydar, don't you? You drink in every word he says!"

This wasn't true. Thaydar spent as much time holding babies and repeating himself as Seylin did. He was just more philosophical about it.

"Thaydar isn't rude," Emily replied tartly.

"Rude? I'm rude? You never even listen to me, but that's not rude."

"I heard every word!" cried Emily. "You want to talk, you won't be a guard, you don't want to be anything, and I don't care. All you ever do is complain. Thaydar never does."

"Well, why don't you just marry Thaydar, since you're so fond of him?" he demanded.

"I certainly wouldn't marry you," declared the wrathful Emily. "Not if you were the last goblin on earth."

Seylin stared at her, his anger evaporating.

"Do you mean that?" he asked incredulously.

Emily was still furious. "Of course I do," she snapped, rising and catching the little boy as he made a dash for the terrace. Seylin stood up and stared after her for a minute, but she didn't turn around to look at him.

"Fine," he said bitterly. "Marry Thaydar, then." And he stormed out of the apartment.

◦—

Seylin found the goblin King in his workroom, giving his wife her magic lesson. The young man stopped in the doorway to watch, bending down to give Kate's drowsy dog a pat and exchanging a quiet greeting with the guard on duty in the hall.

The goblin King's Wife had required years of convincing before she had agreed to learn magic. She always felt uneasy about what her father would have said about it. Kate had been raised a perfect English gentlewoman, and she had been shocked to learn that her great-great-grandmother was an elf. Even though she was technically an elf-human cross, she was so strongly elvish that the goblins called her an elf, too.

Kate no longer noticed that her husband looked alarming, but the first sight of Marak had been enough to startle her into hysterics. The goblin King's body was powerful and bowlegged, with long, wiry arms and big, knotted hands. His magic hand had six fingers. His face was broad and bony, with sunken temples and deep eye sockets, and the eyes that gleamed brightly from under his bushy eyebrows were two different colors, one green and one black. Marak's skin was pale gray, and his lips and fingernails were a rather gruesome shade of dark tan. His hair was as coarse and straight as a horse's tail.

Kate still noticed that hair. It fell in an unruly shock to his shoulders and into his eyes, and he had the habit of running his hands through it as he thought. Most of it was light beige, but a black patch grew back in a cowlick above his green eye, sending strands of black hair falling over the pale hair in what looked like long stripes. Kate disapproved of anything so untidy and kept their young son's hair short as a precaution against his developing his father's taste in hairstyles.

For this lesson, Kate was learning how to heat an elvish cooking stone. The nocturnal elves saw perfectly well in the dark but were blind in the dazzling day. Their eyes were even more sensitive than those of the goblins, so they cooked on special stones that gave off no light. The dwarves had made such a stone for Marak, flat and about a foot square. It lay now on the floor at Kate's feet, and a small metal pan full of water sat on it, waiting to be heated.

"You remember what I taught you about heat spells," Marak said, catching sight of Seylin and motioning for him not to disturb Kate. "They're based in Nameshda, the Warrior constellation, and they focus on the Foot Star. Find the constellation in your mind and point to it." Kate, eyes closed, pointed toward the floor by the writing desk. "That's right, it hasn't risen, so you need to get a good connection even though the ground is in the way. Reach to the Foot Star with one hand and with the other toward the stone as you say the spell. You should be able to feel the heat move by you on its way into the stone. Don't try to do too much. Less is better than more."

Kate nodded and moved her other hand into position. Marak watched as her lips moved and then looked down to examine the pan of water.

Seylin saw several things happen almost at once. Marak stepped back, throwing out his hand and giving a shout. All the water in the pan rushed up in a cloud of steam and whirled toward the King. When it reached his outstretched hand, the cloud splashed against an invisible wall and became a sheet of ice that fell to the floor and shattered. The metal pan melted with a sigh onto the stone, which was turning an alarming shade of cherry red.

Marak shouted again, but Kate stood oblivious, hands still outstretched. With a zing, the painted golden snake around her neck awoke and looped itself about her arms, jerking them to her sides. Marak bent and touched the stone, instantly chilling it. It cracked into several pieces, and the melted pan solidified into a flattened disk with the handle still extending from its side.

"What happened?" asked Kate curiously, opening her eyes.

Marak didn't look up. He was studying the wreckage of the cooking stone and pan, running his hand through his impossible hair. The golden snake twined back up to her shoulders and surveyed the damage, too.

"Forty-seven King's Wives have tried to kill the King," it whispered calmly, "but only eight have tried to kill the King with elf magic." Seylin noticed a hint of complacent pride in the snake's sibilant voice.

"Charm, you know perfectly well I didn't try to kill the King!" said Kate in dismay. The snake looped around to study her innocent blue eyes. Then it let out a gentle hiss and collapsed back into painted sleep.

"Oh, yes, you did, you bloodthirsty elf," replied Marak. "It's the Nameshda spells. Every time you've attempted a spell centered on the Warrior constellation, you've done some kind of damage. We don't need to wonder what your family did for the elf King, Kate. They were high-ranking military lords who devoted their lives to butchering goblins. When you make contact with the Warrior constellation, your proud elf blood burns, and you want to wrap your hands around the nearest goblin throat you can find."

"That's completely ridiculous!" exclaimed Kate. "Isn't it?" she added uncertainly.

For answer, Marak pried the pan off the shattered stone and held it out to her.

"Do I lie?" he pointed out. "No more Nameshda spells for you. Seylin, you can see why the King has to be the one to teach magic to outsiders. They can be very unpredictable and dangerous."

He put the pan on his writing desk and studied his petite, golden-haired wife for a minute. She certainly didn't look dangerous.

"No defense spells of any kind, Kate—they'll only strengthen your warrior tendencies. It's risky when the magic begins teaching itself like that. No more lessons this week, and we'd better calm down your right hand for a few days to prevent accidents. Your magic is excited now, and it will want more blood."

He took Kate's hand in both of his, the two right hands palm to palm, and stood motionless for a minute, frowning in concentration. After a few seconds, Kate tried to pull away.

"Ow!" she said. "Ow! Marak, you're hurting me!"

The goblin ignored her as he finished the magic. Then he looked down at her distressed face with a smile.

"That was your fault," he said. "You didn't want to give that power up, you elf assassin. You fought me to keep it. What killers your people must have been," he added, surveying her with fond pride. "It's lovely goblin revenge against your ancestors that I have you down here with me."

Kate poked at her hand, scowling. "My whole arm's gone numb," she complained.

"And a very good thing, too," remarked the King, rubbing it for her. "I can't have you attacking our son the next time he comes running up to you. He's a little young to understand why his mother would try to kill him, and I think his defense magic would catch you by surprise."

"Marak!" exclaimed Kate. "I'd better not learn magic at all, then. I don't want to hurt anybody."

"Other than me, you mean?" laughed her husband. "Don't fret. We'll just have to find something else you're good at besides killing people. Seylin, did you need to see me?"

Kate kissed her husband good-bye and walked off down the hallway, still rubbing her arm. The dog stood up, stretching luxuriously from her front feet to her back feet, and trotted off after her mistress.

Marak sat down at his desk and waved the young man to a stool. Seylin had always been Marak's special protégé, sharing the King's fascination with unusual magic, but he required a particular sort of handling. He wasn't like a goblin in his nature. He was sensitive and easily upset by things, the effect of his strongly dominant elf blood. Marak could see that he was upset now.

"Goblin King, I'm here to ask permission to leave the kingdom," divulged the miserable Seylin.

Marak's astonishment didn't show on his face. "When will you be coming back?" he asked.

"I don't know." Seylin sighed. "I don't think I will be coming back. I don't think there's much of a place for me here. I'm so different. I want to go live with my own people."

"Your own people," mused Marak, his unmatched eyes shrewd, and the ghost of a smirk on his face. "Which people are those?"

The unhappy young man dropped his gaze and studied his hands in awkward silence.

"Seylin," said Marak, "tell me what's wrong because it's something serious. At least, it had better be."

"I proposed to Em, and she rejected me," muttered Seylin. "She said she wants to marry Thaydar."

Marak stared at and through him, concentrating on the news. Emily and his wife were sisters, but Emily had almost no elvish blood at all. The goblins called her a human. She had come to the kingdom voluntarily in order to be with her sister, and Marak had promised her that she would be allowed to choose her own husband one day. Emily and Seylin got along so well together that Marak had been sure of her choice, but here she was, picking a real goblin's goblin over twice her age. With that kind of taste, Marak thought, she'd have been a good King's Wife.

"So now you want to find an elf bride," he concluded. Seylin colored up in embarrassment.

"I don't know about that," he answered. "I just want to find some elves."

"What makes you think there are elves to find?" demanded Marak. "The last elf King has been dead for over two hundred years, and when he died, the elvish race died, too."

"The goblins never did track down every last elf," observed Seylin. "Some of the elf lords moved away during the elf harrowing, along with groups of refugees."

"Marak Whiteye knew that they were finished," countered the King. "Most of the elf men died in battle. Their widows poured into the camps that remained, and there weren't enough hunters to feed them. They were starving to death. Whiteye didn't need to hunt them down."

"Kate's ancestor survived it," noted Seylin. "And if she did, so could others."

"Kate's ancestor had to marry a human man because her own people were dead, and she herself died almost a hundred years ago. These arguments don't convince me, Seylin. Why are they convincing you?"

The young man frowned at his hands again. He didn't look up as he spoke.

"I have a feeling about it. A feeling. That's all. We were coming back from the trading journey when I first noticed it. One night, I sensed that elves were near me in the forest. I almost felt pulled out of my skin. I've been restless ever since. It was like a call."

"A call." The King's eyes blazed with excitement. "I always knew you were born elvish for a reason. It's your magic—or it's wishful thinking. I don't know which. So now you want to go find your elves. And if you find them, are you going to tell your King about them?"

"Well . . ." Seylin blushed again. "I don't think they'd want me to. And I wouldn't want them to . . . to come to harm . . . because of me."

"Come to harm?" echoed Marak contemptuously. "Seylin, stop thinking like an elf! You are who you are, and I am who I am because elf brides 'came to harm.' You just saw an elf bride not five minutes ago. Would you say that Kate came to harm?"

"It can't matter," protested Seylin. "There must be so few elves left, if any. They need their own brides, or there won't be any more elves at all."

"An excellent point," agreed Marak. "But you're not willing to leave the decision up to my good judgment?"

The young man didn't answer.

"Oh, Seylin, you're confused," said Marak, chuckling. "Living with your people! You've spent too many years looking at your pretty face in the mirror."

In the silence that followed, the goblin King considered the proposed quest. It had possibilities, but that elf nature had to be free to do the hunting. Treat Seylin like a goblin, and the chance would be gone. Quite a chance for Seylin, quite a chance for the goblins. Maybe even a chance for the elves.

"Very well, I give you permission to hunt for elves," he said finally. "And here's what I can do for you and *your* people. I won't order anyone to follow you, and I won't authorize any goblin to contact the elves you may find. I will authorize no raids for brides, and I won't ask that you report to me. I will contact you, but I'll do it in such a way that your elf friends won't know, and you will be free to answer me or not. I won't ask that you return to the kingdom, either, although I do hope that someday you will."

Seylin felt a profound relief. He had been worried about leading goblins to an elf colony, but now he could live among his people with a clear conscience.

"There are only two conditions," added Marak dispassionately. "First, you are and always will be my subject, and I will not allow one of my subjects to suffer attack. If anyone attacks you, even an elf, I have the right to protect you and take revenge. The day—no, the second—that you suffer violent harm at the hands of an elf, I cancel all my promises. That's my obligation to you as your King because you are one of *my* people."

"That seems fair," remarked the young man. "I can't imagine anyone attacking me." The goblin King just smiled at him. He knew Seylin couldn't imagine it.

"And the second condition," he said, getting up and crossing to a drawer, "is that I need a lock of your hair and three drops of blood." He returned with a pair of scissors, a small plate, and an object that looked like a golden tack.

"Why?" demanded Seylin, immediately attracted by the thought of the magic.

"If I told you it's a keepsake, would you believe me?" chuckled Marak. He cut off one of Seylin's black locks and arranged it carefully into a ring on the plate. Then, frowning absently, he stuck the young man's finger and squeezed three drops onto the hair.

"It's a tracking spell," guessed Seylin, "so you'll know where I am. That's good. I'm glad you'll be looking after me."

"Seylin, Seylin," Marak chided. "You can't wait to leave here and find *your* people, but you're glad *your* King is looking after you. I don't know what will come from such a puzzle, but I'm anxious to find out. Here," he added, reaching for paper and writing a short note, "give this to the storeroom clerks, and they'll provide you with anything you need. Happy hunting for your people, but don't stay away too long. Your King hopes that you'll be back home with us soon."

After his unhappy subject left, Marak sat at his desk for an hour, working intently over the lock of hair, weaving three different colors of waxed thread around it to seal it inside a braided ring.

"Guard, come!" he called, putting the finished ring into a drawer, and Tinsel appeared in the doorway. Tinsel wasn't excessively tall, but he seemed like a giant because of his broad build, and his skin was a dull silver-gray. His silver hair was the most startling thing about him. It looked like something the dwarves had made, and the light glittering on it almost hurt the eyes.

The goblin King surveyed his guard thoughtfully. Here was another strongly dominant elf cross, he thought to himself, rather good-looking as goblins went, with no distinctive deformities. Blue or silver skin often showed up when strong elf blood hit goblin blood, and often the strong elf crosses had those blue eyes. Tinsel would have been a good match for Emily's age and elf ancestry, too, almost as good a match as Seylin. Marak studied the young guard a bit moodily. He'd have been a better match than Thaydar.

"Now, why haven't you been trying for young M yourself?" growled the King. "A handsome brute like you."

"Who, me?" asked Tinsel. "Thaydar and Seylin are both after her. Seylin and I were pages together, and Thaydar's my boss." He smiled his good-natured, slightly goofy smile. "That kind of trouble I don't need."

No, he wouldn't, considered Marak with a sigh. He'd find no fiercely competitive spirit here. Goblins generally got along, but Tinsel was beyond the pale. Remarkable for the calmness of his temper, he was just tremendously nice. This had led to a certain amount of teasing when he was a page, but Tinsel had developed a unique solution. He had picked up the tormentor and carried him around until the child promised to leave him alone.

"Go find M for me, Tinsel," said Marak resignedly. "I need to talk to her. I'll be in my rooms." He walked downstairs, thinking it over. Thaydar, of all goblins, and his Seylin gone from the kingdom entirely. He couldn't wait to hear Emily's side of this one.

He sat down in his favorite reading chair and pulled *A History of the Kings of England* out of the bookcase. Over the years, the goblins who went out on trading journeys had brought Kate a number of books. She used them to teach the pages their English, and she read them for pleasure. Marak read them as much as she did. He thought that a careful king should study those peoples whose lands bordered his own. He always picked this particular book when he was depressed about kingdom concerns; it cheered him up to see how horribly the human kings managed.

Kate lay on a couch nearby, her arm wrapped in a blanket and her lips moving as she read the book of elvish spells they were working through. She couldn't do the magic this week, but she could at least study. A companionable silence settled over the room.

"Do you know, Kate," murmured Marak after a while, "I don't believe these people have kings at all. Not a one of them does any healing or worries about the food crops."

Kate glanced up, trying to pay attention to her husband while remembering that deer health was governed by the Gilim constellation. She had always thought that elf magic would be about pretty things. It amazed her that so many of the spells had to do with deer.

"Of course we have kings," she answered firmly, good English citizen that she was. "Marak, what's the Gilim constellation? I can't place it."

"It's the Milky Way," he replied absently. "Gilim means 'herd'; to the elves it looked like a herd of deer crossing a glade."

"Herd." Kate digested this. "I like 'Milky Way' better. It sounds so much more romantic."

"Really?" Marak laughed. "I didn't know there was anything romantic about having a pan of milk spilled over your head." With a frown, Kate went back to her spell book.

Emily hurried into the room without knocking, and Marak put down his book.

"Finally, M," he commented. "I've had Tinsel looking for you."

"Never mind about that," said Emily breathlessly. "Marak, you have to do something! Brindle said that Seylin went off on a trip, and he told Brindle he isn't coming back."

This looked like kingdom business, Kate decided, and she left the room to prepare for the day's English classes. Emily had gotten into plenty of scrapes and adventures over the years, and she and Marak had had many heated discussions. Kate was glad to stay out of them whenever she could.

"Yes, that's true," remarked Marak calmly. "Seylin asked me for permission to leave."

"But you can't let him leave like that!" said Emily. "Seylin can't just go away and not come back. Or maybe—maybe I could go with him," she suggested, brightening.

"M, you are not going with him," answered the goblin King. "He left the kingdom just to get away from you."

"From me?" echoed Emily, sitting down on the couch. She stared at him in amazement. "But why?"

"Congratulations on your choice of a husband," said Marak by way of reply. "I know how pleased Thaydar must be. I haven't talked to him yet, but I'm sure you have. I'd like to hold the wedding as soon as possible."

Emily gaped at him.

"I don't want to marry Thaydar!" she exclaimed.

The goblin King returned her gaze impassively. "Didn't you tell Seylin today that you wanted to marry Thaydar?"

Emily tried to remember their conversation.

"Well, yes and no," she answered. "I told him that I'd rather marry Thaydar than him, but only because he was being so rude. He made Brindle's little Penelope cry because he wouldn't change into a cat."

The goblin King's face lit up with amusement. "Seylin was proposing marriage to you," he cried, "and you wanted him to change into a *cat*?"

"Marriage?" gasped Emily. "He never mentioned marriage! He said that he wouldn't always be a guard, and he didn't have much to offer, but— Oh . . ." She trailed off, stunned.

Marak was helpless with laughter.

"Oh," he agreed when he recovered, wiping his eyes. "You certainly conveyed a clear refusal, anyway, as well as a clear preference for Thaydar. M, I told you that you were free to choose your own husband, and it's high time. Cats aside, which man do you want to marry?"

Emily continued to look dazed.

"I don't really know," she confessed. "I don't want to marry anybody. Why do I have to?"

Her brother-in-law rested his cheek on his hand and studied her affectionately. "What would you have said to Seylin if you'd known he was proposing?"

Emily shrugged. "I don't know," she admitted reluctantly. "I don't want Seylin to go away and not come back. But he's been the worst nuisance this year, standing around and goggling at me. He's never been less fun."

"Seylin finally realized that he loved you," pointed out the goblin King.

"Well, he didn't act like he loved me," complained the young woman. "All he did was grumble at me and act embarrassed. Why does it have to be like this? We were always such good friends."

Because sooner or later we all grow up, Marak reflected, and I should have known that Seylin would do it first. Lighthearted Emily was showing no real interest in growing up. It was time to give her a shove in the right direction.

"M, I have bad news," he announced. "Seylin thinks you're marrying Thaydar, so he's left the kingdom to find an elf bride. I'm afraid you'll have to put him completely out of your mind."

"An elf bride! There aren't any elves left!" protested the girl.

"Seylin thinks there are," observed Marak. "He thinks he almost met some, and I wouldn't be surprised if he's right. He doesn't intend to return, so he's no longer a suitable choice for you. I'll give you a couple of months to decide on a goblin man you'd prefer, and if you can't do that, I'll marry you to Thaydar. You expressed a preference for him, however briefly."

Emily stared at him in astonishment.

"But—but—Marak!" she spluttered.

"Seylin's quest is very important," cautioned her brother-in-law. "I refuse to allow you to interfere. Don't waste your time thinking about him. He has better things to do than remember past sweethearts, and so do you."

"I'm *past*?" exclaimed Emily furiously. "Me? *Past?*"

"I'm glad that's settled," commented Marak, standing up. "Time for court. As soon as you have that name, I'll be pleased to hear it."

He left, and Emily sat there, feeling completely stunned. So that was where Seylin had gone! He wanted to find an elf girl. Someone prettier than she was. Someone magical and fascinating. He didn't even care about her.

Meanwhile, Seylin huddled in the woods of Hallow Hill, in the black cat shape that Emily loved. Probably Marak had already performed the wedding ceremony, he thought. Probably she was kissing Thaydar right this minute. She'd found herself a real goblin. She didn't even care about him.

chapter Two

Kate was waiting for her husband in the hallway outside their rooms, and they walked downstairs together.

"What's all this about Seylin leaving?" she wanted to know.

"M didn't notice that he was proposing to her," explained Marak. "Think of that—she didn't even notice! Seylin wanted to follow an odd feeling he's had and go away to hunt for elves. He thinks she's decided to marry Thaydar."

"That doesn't sound like a good match," said Kate unhappily.

"I don't know," mused Marak. "It's not the one I would have wanted, but my military commander is amazingly patient. And he's trained for combat situations." Kate didn't laugh.

"Poor Seylin!" she said. "He must be so mortified, he'll never come back home. And he'll certainly never consider asking her to marry him again. I don't think Em is at all suited to Thaydar. They'll make each other completely miserable."

"That's the most likely result," agreed Marak happily. Kate gave him a surprised glance. He was scheming again. There was nothing the clever goblin loved more than an impossibly tangled problem. "How's the arm?" he asked.

"It's better," she assured him as he felt and flexed it. "It tingles every now and then, that's all."

"Poor little elf! Elves who attack the goblin King never win," he said. "Speaking of battles, did you choose a roommate for Til? The new pages move into their rooms in a few weeks."

"Yes, I did," answered his wife. Her magical snake, Charm, had named the little girl Kate had rescued from the sorcerer's lair Matilda, but they had called her Til almost from the start. "We thought Bony's oldest girl would be a good choice. It's going to be such a hard adjust-ment for Til."

"It's going to be a hard adjustment for the pages," remarked the goblin King. "That girl is even worse than M was. She's a terror."

"She's young," countered Kate. Her voice was sad. "Marak, don't you think she's too young to leave us?"

"No, I don't, and neither do you. Kate, every mother in the high families goes through this. All the pages move to the pages' floor; that's how they make important friendships."

"But Catspaw!" objected Kate, thinking of her young goblin son. "He'll miss her so. They've never been apart."

"They've never stopped fighting, either. His magic's developing so fast, he'll probably wind up killing her if we don't separate them. He's already singed her hair off twice, and last week I caught him changing her into a duck."

Kate left Marak outside the great throne room. Court began, and the stately room buzzed with well-dressed goblins. Marak was listen-ing patiently to a complaint against one of the dwarves who lived in the palace when Emily appeared at the edge of the crowd.

"That dwarf's been moving the wall between our apartments a little bit each day," declared a goblin. "My bedroom keeps getting smaller and smaller. The furniture won't fit."

"Rubbish!" scoffed the dwarf. "I never did." Emily maneuvered until she was right behind him and began gesturing significantly to Marak.

"Did you measure your bedroom?" the King inquired of the goblin.

"I did, but the tape measure's metal, so it does just what he wants! The numbers keep getting closer together, but the measurement stays the same. And there's barely room for the bed now. My clothes are in the hall!"

Marak turned to the dwarf, but Emily had shouldered past him. "I have to talk to you!" she whispered frantically.

"Just a moment," the goblin King said graciously to the crowd, and he escorted the young woman from the dais. He opened the door of a small anteroom and motioned her inside.

"Why do you insist on interrupting me while I'm holding court?" he demanded.

"It's important," pleaded Emily. "Marak, just this once!"

"It isn't just this once. Every few weeks I look up and there you are, hopping around as if you have an incurable twitch."

"But it's urgent! I need to speak to you as soon as possible!"

"All right," promised the goblin King. "I'll be back as soon as possible." He left her in the anteroom and locked the door. Three hours later, he unlocked it again. "Now, why did you need to speak to me?"

Emily was sitting on the floor unraveling a gold tassel. She glared at her brother-in-law.

"As soon as possible? I could have died in here!"

"I don't see how," he remarked thoughtfully, looking around the room. "And I couldn't possibly see you until court was over. We had a very busy morning. You've been crying," he added, pleased to have noticed. He had learned to detect these sorts of things during the eight years that the sisters had been in his underground realm.

"Of course not," said Emily tartly, and the goblin let the matter pass. "Marak, I want to go outside the kingdom, but for some reason the iron doors won't let me out."

"I told them not to," he replied. "Why do you need to go out?"

"I want to spend some time outside the kingdom, and I don't see why I shouldn't be allowed to."

"How long?" asked Marak.

Emily hesitated. "I don't know. Maybe just a few days. Or maybe longer. It depends on how long things take."

"A quest?"

Emily nodded.

"What a remarkable coincidence! Two quests in one day. What exactly are you going to find?"

"My human nature," replied Emily solemnly. She had practiced for this moment. She sat in dignified silence while the goblin King laughed.

"Your human nature?" he hooted. "You won't have to look very far! Why do you persist in lying to me when you know I can tell?"

"I'm not lying," asserted the girl. "Allow me to quote to you from that indispensable manual, *The Care and Maintenance of Human Brides*." She produced the battered old volume from behind her back.

"You've been rifling through my workroom again," observed Marak, and his voice had a dangerous edge. During Emily's checkered career with the pages, she had sat through many a tense moment with her brother-in-law, and she knew every dangerous edge his voice possessed. This one was only annoyance. She decided to ignore it.

"'The human bride should, if possible, be left in her natural surroundings until maturity,'" she intoned. "'This allows the distinctive nature of her race the full time to develop. If called into the kingdom too quickly, she loses the opportunity to try her human traits in their proper setting. Her subsequent strength of character may be diminished.'" She put down the book and gazed severely at the goblin. "You didn't do that with me."

Marak grinned. "And just look at your weakness of character! M, this is absurd, and you know it. Give me back my book, and stay out of my workroom."

The young woman handed over the book, struggling to control herself.

"It isn't absurd!" she insisted. "I've lived down here so long, I don't remember what it's like outside. I want to go see it again. I've lost something out there. It's something I want, Marak. Or something I think I want. I need to find it again. I need to find out."

The goblin King pushed his hair out of his face and paused for a moment, deep in thought. "What if you don't find what you're looking for?" he asked.

Emily's face fell. She hadn't considered defeat. She never did.

"I'll come back and get married," she said. "To anybody."

Her brother-in-law studied her shrewdly.

"M, there's something you need to know," he said, choosing his words with care. "If you go hunting outside, you'll find what I want you to find. And nothing more. Do you understand?"

"Yes," she muttered. "But I still want to try."

"All right. You can try. But I'll have to send someone with you. You don't have a shred of magic to protect you out there."

Emily brightened a little. "Tinsel could go."

"And Tinsel could fall into line with any idiotic plan you think up. Tinsel's too nice, and he's never been a match for your clever talk. None of your page friends have been, for that matter. I'll send someone else. You may leave tomorrow morning. Come see me in the workroom right after breakfast; I need to work some tracking magic. Then I'll let you out. I'll have your escort waiting in the guardroom with an adequate pack."

"But—what's wrong with leaving this evening?" demanded Emily, mentally calculating how far Seylin might have traveled. "It won't take that long to get ready, and the trading carts always leave at night."

"M, you don't want to live like a goblin," reproved Marak, his eyes bright. "Up at dawn, that's how your people live. Remember, you're seeking your human nature." His shouts of laughter followed her as she stomped off down the hall.

Emily hardly slept that night. It didn't matter that Marak had laughed at her. The goblin King had fallen for her arguments, and Seylin was as good as found. He would be upset at first, of course, but a few well-chosen words and he would see that it was all non-sense. Better yet, she could make him see that it was all his fault, and he would give up the idea of an elf bride. Once back in the king-dom, she could stall them both on the marriage issue. Not that it would be such a bad idea to marry Seylin eventually, but having to talk over every plan with another person before you did anything sounded awfully boring. Married people were always so serious.

In the morning, the goblin King was perfectly cordial. As he cut a lock of her hair and pricked her finger, he delivered a few words of advice on life in the human world. Emily didn't pay any attention. She wouldn't be in the human world very long. She asked him discreet questions about Seylin's quest instead, and he was surprisingly coop-erative. He told her about Seylin's odd feeling while he was on his trad-ing journey and about the promises Marak had made not to interfere.

"I told him I wouldn't order anyone to follow him," he observed. "I informed the assembly at breakfast about his search for elves and forbade them to contact the elves he may find. You should have been there. You would have learned more than you're learning now, and you would have started your journey with a decent meal."

"I'm not hungry," she assured him absently. The goblins were ordered not to contact any elves, she noticed, but that didn't mean they couldn't contact Seylin. Her escort might protest this course of action, but she would soon talk him around. Goblins were entirely too docile, she reflected. The King's magic didn't allow them to disobey.

"Enjoy your quest," he said as he solicitously healed the pin-prick. "I suppose I should wish you good luck."

Emily smiled. "My luck has always been good," she informed him.

Marak smiled back. Amusement glinted in his odd-colored eyes, but, then, he was always amused about something.

"Who are you sending with me?" she wanted to know.

"Someone I can count on," he answered vaguely. "A good companion for a quest in the human world."

Emily should have been more suspicious.

She left her monkey in the care of a fellow page and hurried to the guardroom. It was empty except for one short, heavyset figure wearing a voluminous black cloak, leaning over and rummaging in a large pack. The figure straightened up and turned around, and Emily let out a howl of dismay.

"EM!" The voice screeched like a knife blade scratching slate. "What is this nonsense about your trudging around outside on some ridiculous hunt? This is one of your sly tricks again, isn't it? Well? Answer me!"

The woman peering accusingly at Emily had translucent light green skin, and Emily had once told another page that she was as wide as she was tall. Her eyes were so pale that the pupil and a dark gray ring at the edge of the iris were their only color. The goblins called them white eyes, and their stare was disagreeably mesmerizing. Her mouth was very broad and lipless, rather like that of a frog, with large yellow teeth that leaned to and fro at odd angles. Her hair, strangely enough, was as beautiful as Kate's: golden, curling locks that she wore pulled back in a modest bun. The whole effect of her appearance was dismally unpleasant. She was simply too ugly for words.

"Ruby! I can't believe it!" exclaimed Emily. She turned to the silent walls. "Marak!" she cried. "Is this your idea of a joke?"

"I'll thank you to call me Lore-Master Ruby, you little minx," snapped the woman. "And I don't want to hear any more disrespectful complaints against our King."

Ruby's charming name had nothing to do with the gemstone; it was very close to the goblin word for "teacher." Her happy parents had given her the name after the midwife had detected a strong talent for this profession in their newborn. Ruby was one of many goblin women with no interest in marriage. She had been teaching, according to the pages, since the Dawn of Time. She devoted herself wholeheartedly to the education of young minds, and no teacher ever worked harder, but generations of wretched pages wished that she hadn't.

To say that she was Emily's least favorite teacher would be a dreadful understatement. It would be more accurate to say that she was Emily's most hated teacher. Lore-Master Ruby was an expert who taught about all things human, and she knew her subject inside and out. Her classes were the most thorough and her tests were the most difficult of any that the pages encountered. But one fact was abundantly clear, from the very first lesson to the last word on the very last test: Lore-Master Ruby absolutely loathed the human race.

Emily and Ruby had fought for years. Their battlefield was the classroom, and the other pages were the fascinated spectators. Ruby relished the opportunity to point out the inferiorities of humans, and Emily, with her inattentiveness, her quarrelsome nature, and her shrewd manner, was an ideal example.

By trial and error, Emily had found the perfect revenge. Day after day, she ignored the lessons, reading her own books during class. She never once did the assignments or turned in any homework. But she earned a perfect score on every one of Ruby's fabulously hard tests. None of the other goblins ever managed it. Only Seylin even came close.

Ruby ground her yellow teeth with rage over those perfect scores, which made all her careful teaching seem unnecessary. She knew how Emily would gloat the next day in class. "It's so easy," she would say cheerfully to the other pages, showing off her test. "But I suppose it's one of those things only a human can do."

Now Emily faced her foe again in the empty guardroom. "Did the King actually choose you to accompany me?" she demanded.

"He did. He said it was most important. Please don't imagine that I volunteered."

"And if I complain, he'll just tell me to stay home." Emily gave an exasperated sigh. "Oh, very well. Let's go. If my luck holds, we'll be back before nightfall."

But Emily's good luck had vanished. She found no sign of Seylin in the forest outside and couldn't determine which way he had gone. Day after day, she searched for him while her former teacher scolded and grumbled. The goblin kingdom was a small, tidy place. She had forgotten how big the human world could be. Every road stretched on forever. Finding one young man in that vast expanse began to seem impossible.

Meanwhile, Marak paused every day to consult two maps that he had fastened to the wall of his workroom. One showed Seylin's wanderings, and the other showed Emily's progress. Hanging on two hooks next to the maps were the braided rings made from their hair. Marak smiled as he took down Emily's ring and held it in his palm.

"The scholars say that persistence is one of the most basic human traits," he told it. "We're going to find out if that's true."

chapter Three

Seylin retraced his former trading journey, but no call came to tell him that elves were nearby. Before the death of the last elf King, several thousand elves had lived in eighteen camps scattered through the elf King's forest. Each camp had contained as many as two hundred and fifty people under the guidance of a camp lord. The nomadic elves had moved from location to location throughout the year, but the camps had retained a precise pattern in relation to each other. They had formed the shape of the Warrior constellation, with the King's camp in the center.

Now Seylin spent weeks combing the elf King's silent forest for the remains of the camps. He found ancient sites that had been used by the elves for thousands of years, but no sign showed that anyone had been near them in perhaps a century.

Failing to find elves in the forest, he began to spend more time in the little human villages that dotted the edge of the elf King's old domain. He told himself that this was a prudent decision because the humans might have some information for him, but the fact of the matter was that he was lonely. Goblins were very gregarious. They lived and ate together, worked together, went on patrol together, and visited one another almost constantly.

Seylin had been alone for several weeks now, and he began to prefer any companionship to that. But because humans were only out during the day, he couldn't have very much contact with them. In the twilit evenings, he could sit inside the public houses over a beer, or he could change into a cat and watch humans going about their daylight business from the cover of nearby bushes.

One morning, Seylin decided to stay up for a while and do some people-watching. Before dawn, he came to a little town and found a deserted shed right next to the forest. He hid his pack carefully behind some old junk, changed into a cat, and strolled out into the early morning. He headed down a weedy garden path toward the ramshackle old house that his shed belonged to. Perhaps some people inside were awake over their breakfasts, although he rather doubted it. If the shed and garden were any indication, they weren't the industrious sort.

"You're a cat now!" exclaimed a voice behind him, and Seylin bounded into the air. A thin girl emerged from a bush and pushed back straggly fair hair, her pale cheeks flushed with excitement. "You're under an enchantment, aren't you?" she demanded breathlessly.

Seylin twitched his bottle brush tail as he considered what to do. The child, only about nine or ten, didn't look dangerous, and she was talking about things he understood. His tail died back to a soft fluff again, and he sat down in the garden weeds.

"Yes, I am under an enchantment," he confirmed in his high cat voice.

The skinny little wraith before him didn't even blink at this extraordinary news, and she didn't look surprised to hear him speak, either. She just clasped her hands together and walked up to him, her face ecstatic.

"Oh, I just knew it!" she cried. "I'll help you if you like. You could marry me when I grow up, and then you would have to leave me and be locked away in the farthest castle, and I would wander looking for you for seven years, over mountain and valley, and finally find you about to marry the troll princess, and I would trade my ring to talk to you, but you would be in a magical sleep, and I'd sit by you and cry and say, 'I've sought you for seven years,' and a tear would fall on your cheek and wake you up, and then the enchantment would be broken."

Seylin stared at the excited little girl with his golden eyes. "That sounds like a lot of trouble," he said politely. "I think I'll just stay a cat, if it's all the same to you."

"Well, you do make a nice cat," she went on enthusiastically. "May I pet you?" And she sat down beside him and tickled him under the chin. Seylin started to purr. Usually he tried not to do this because it struck him as undignified, but he couldn't help himself. After an entire fruitless month of roaming through the woods, it was nice to be tickled under the chin.

"Who enchanted you?" she asked. "Was it an evil witch disguised as a beautiful red-haired woman, or was it some fairy who hated your family? Are you really a prince? Where's your kingdom?"

Seylin puzzled over this. It was obvious to him that they had both studied magic, but from very different books.

"No, I'm not a prince," he told her. "I enchanted myself. I can't change back right now because the light would hurt my eyes."

"Oh," she said, a little disappointed. "Most people under enchantments are handsome princes." She told him several stories to prove her point. Seylin listened with interest. He supposed that they were possible, but a lot of the magic seemed terribly impractical.

"How do you know all this?" he asked. "Where did you learn about magic?"

"My father told me some of them, and I've read some of them in books," she said. "My father knows everything. He used to be almost a prince himself and lived in a richly appointed house filled with servants who obeyed his every command. But then he met my mother, and even though they weren't supposed to speak to each other, she won his heart with her enchanting beauty. His evil mother tried to separate them, and she cast my mother out of doors to starve, but my wise and handsome father rescued her and took her away to marry. They should have lived happily ever after," the thin little girl said seriously, "but when I was a baby, my mother wasted away and died, and my father wandered about with me, penniless and in terrible distress. Sometimes he gives lessons to the little boys in the town, but most of the time he's too sick with a broken heart to get out of bed, so I have to tell them to go away."

The two unlikely companions spent a happy morning together. The little girl talked, and Seylin listened. Her name was Jane, and she confessed that she was unhappy about this because she had never read a single story about a beautiful maiden named Jane. Seylin decided that she wasn't going to be a beautiful maiden anyway. She was a plain little thing, scrawny and a bit dirty, with clothes that were too small for her. It gradually dawned on Seylin that he was enjoying her company because she reminded him of Emily. This depressed him, and he remembered that he hadn't had any sleep.

"I need to leave now," he said. The little girl looked crushed.

"Don't leave," she implored him. "I can't bear to say good-bye. You haven't told me anything about your enchantment yet, or what it's like to be a cat. I still don't know if you eat mice, and I don't know how to find your kingdom. I don't know why you put a curse on yourself, and why your eyes would hurt if you didn't. You can't just go!"

Seylin was tired from walking night after night, and he hadn't met any other human who seemed to care for magic. Perhaps this little girl could help him, or perhaps her father could. He would rest up for a day or two. He'd probably have to walk for months yet.

"I really do need to leave," he said, "but maybe you'll see me again. Don't tell anyone about me, or I won't be able to come back."

"Oh, I won't," she promised solemnly. "Just like the lovely golden-haired princess who couldn't speak, and the witch smeared blood on her face, and her husband the king came and said, 'Where's our baby?' and she couldn't say a single solitary word."

"Something like that," agreed Seylin. What little he'd learned about the local human kings had sounded rather grim, but he'd had no idea that their lives involved so many strange, magical misadventures.

That night, Seylin came down to the house in order to look through the windows. He had been taught to shun human magic as evil, but the little girl's stories didn't seem evil. Perhaps her father was like the goblin scholars, a man who knew all about the history of human magic without actually practicing it himself. Such a scholar of magic would surely have some idea whether or not elves lived in the area.

But Seylin found his investigations very disappointing. The dilapidated house was a mess inside, and Jane's father didn't appear to be either handsome or wise. He sat at a dirty table, unwashed and unshaved, his clothes rumpled and threadbare, drinking one mug of beer after another until his unhappy face took on a dreamy, stupid look. Seylin watched him for a long time, remembering Jane's odd stories. One thing, at least, was clear to him now: heartache was not the disease keeping this human in bed in the morning.

The next day, Seylin studied the whole area before coming out of the forest. He saw no one stirring, however, except the little girl herself. She was thrilled to see him again and asked scores of questions. Some Seylin answered, but many others he didn't. He refused to tell her anything about his kingdom or his King. He did tell her, however, that he was looking for elves. Jane was very interested in this, but, unfortunately, she didn't know where any might be.

"Why do you have to look for them?" she asked. "Don't you know where they live?"

"Not anymore," Seylin answered. "I hope I can find some of the ones who moved away during the elf harrowing. That was the last war with the goblins," he explained.

"Goblins?" asked Jane eagerly. "Do you know any stories about goblins? Tell me a story about an elf and a goblin."

Seylin loved history and knew dozens of stories. He thought for a minute or two.

"Here's something that happened during the reign of Marak Redeye and Aganir Immir, the elf King named Storm Wind," he said. "One night, the young sister of a great elf lord, the lord of the Third Belt Star Camp, went out with her maidens to dance beneath the moon. She loved more than anything in the world to dance, and she wanted to go to a certain hill where she could dance so high above the quiet forest that she felt as if she were in the sky itself. But the goblins had watched this camp, and they knew her habit. When she and her maidens were far from home, they overpowered her guards and surrounded the terrified elf girls. Then the goblin King himself came, and he let every one of her maidens go, and all the guards, too, but the lord's sister he took underground to be his own bride."

"And was he fearfully ugly?" asked Jane in a hushed voice. "Was he scaly and horrible?"

"Let's see," said Seylin, trying to remember. "No, he wasn't scaly. He had bright red eyes, and he was covered all over with short black fur, like a panther." Jane shivered deliciously.

"The poor elf bride was horrified at her new life in the goblin realm. Gradually her fear died away, but it left behind nothing but sorrow. The goblin King brought her gold and jewels, rich clothes and finery, but none of it mattered to his unhappy wife. She begged instead to be allowed one more night of dancing under the moon, but this he couldn't grant her. She was under a spell never to leave the goblin caves and never to see the night sky again.

"The goblin King's Wife began to pine away, and nothing seemed to help. Again and again, she begged to dance just one more night, and again and again, her husband denied her pleas. Finally, she fell very ill, and then the poor elf girl couldn't have danced even if the King had let her.

"The goblin King sent a message to the lord of the Third Belt Star Camp: 'My wife and your sister lies dying in my kingdom. Send an elf musician to play for her so that she can get well.' When he learned this, the elf lord grieved bitterly, and he called all the musi-cians in his camp to ask if any was brave enough to go down into the goblin caves. One after another turned pale and refused to go, but a young elf man agreed to make that terrible journey. He went with the guards past the great iron door and into the huge palace, and came at last to the room where the poor girl lay, so ill that she didn't even know another elf had braved that trip to come help her.

"Then the goblin King sent his dying wife a beautiful dream of the full moon shining above the hill where he had first found her. The young elf took his pipe and began to play to the sleeping girl. The lovely, haunting elf music flowed into her dream, and she began to dance. So ill that she couldn't even lift her own hand, locked away from the sky that she loved, still, for that one night and in that one dream, the elf girl danced and danced, far from the goblin King, who sat by her bedside and watched the look of joy on her face. The elf piper never stopped playing, and the elf girl never stopped danc-ing, till a full night and day had passed, and evening had come again.

"Then the goblin King said to the piper, 'You have worked very hard playing your pipe for me, but now you won't have to work any longer. I give you the gift of playing the wind itself.' And for the rest of his life, whenever the wind blew, it played all the notes that the piper wished to hear, and he became the most famous musician in the elf kingdom. The goblin King's Wife slept for days and days, tired from all her dancing, and when she finally woke up again, she was sound and well. And there was peace between the elves and goblins for the rest of that King's life."

Jane sat for a minute after Seylin had finished speaking, her thin face puzzled and anxious.

"But, Seylin," she prompted, "that can't be the end of the story."

"Well, I don't know," said the black cat doubtfully. "There never really is an end, is there? I suppose I could say that the elf girl came to love the goblin King very much and that their son, Marak Horsetooth, was one of the greatest of the Kings."

"No, no, no!" said Jane emphatically. "Seylin, that can't be how it ends. She can't love a goblin. Stories just don't turn out like that. Maybe the piper had a magic box with servants in it, and they popped out and killed the goblin King, and then he kissed the elf girl, and she woke up, and they escaped together from the caves, and as a reward for his bravery, the elf lord married her to the piper, and they lived happily ever after."

"That's not possible," protested Seylin. "No elf could kill the goblin King, whether he had servants in a box or not."

"But I want the goblin dead and the poor girl rescued from him!" insisted Jane. "No creature that horrible should live through a story. Change the ending."

"Jane!" cried the cat, his fur bristling. "I told you the truth! Marak Redeye was a good goblin King; he took care of his people, and he loved his wife. It's not the goblins who are dead at all, it's the elves. There's a goblin King alive right this minute, but I don't know if any elves are left."

"That's terrible!" said Jane, folding her arms and refusing to look at him. "The goblins shouldn't be alive and the elves dead. How could you tell me a story like that?"

Seylin thought about all of Jane's stories, in which brave, handsome princes battled witches and trolls, and beautiful maidens lived happily ever after.

"Your stories aren't true, are they?" he observed. "Someone just made them up."

Jane jumped to her feet and faced him indignantly.

"They are, too, true!" she shouted. "They're more true than yours. People really do defeat evil goblins, and they really do live happily ever after!" And she started to cry. Before the surprised Seylin could even speak, she ran into the house and slammed the door.

Seylin spent that night searching the nearby woods for evidence of elves, depressed about his conversation with Jane. He hadn't thought of goblins as such an awful thing, but maybe they really were. Maybe it was wrong that Marak Redeye had saved his wife from dying. Maybe he should have let her die. He remembered his own King telling him, "You are who you are, and I am who I am because elf brides came to harm."

The next morning, he went back to the neglected house to see if Jane would speak to him again. He found her crying in the shed, her messy hair covered with cobwebs.

"You were right, Seylin," she sobbed. "I asked my father, and he told me that the stories weren't true. He says there's no such thing as goblins or elves or happy endings, and that magic doesn't really happen at all."

Seylin curled up next to the white-faced little girl.

"Jane, that's not right, either," he said. "Magic does happen. You're talking to a cat. There are goblins, too, whether your father believes that or not. And there's still one elf left as long as I'm alive."

"But no happy endings!" Jane said. "I just can't bear it." She rubbed her hand across her eyes. They were dull, and her whole manner was different. Seylin felt that it was his fault.

"I hope there are happy endings," he mused. "I'm not sure, but I think I've seen one." He hesitated. "Would you like to see me work some magic? You mustn't ever tell, you know."

Her dirty face lit up.

"I'd love to," she breathed. "When? Now?"

"No," he said. "Elves can't see in the daytime. I'll come back tonight in my normal shape, the way you first saw me. Wait in the woods behind the shed, and I'll take you to see real magic."

That night, the air turned chilly. The cautious young man watched the area for an hour before he came out to greet her. Jane was shivering, and her teeth were chattering, but her eyes were bright with excitement.

Seylin led her to a clearing in the woods and worked all the pretty elf magic he knew for her. He surrounded her with bobbing crescent moons and grew the plant with glowing flowers that had always entranced Emily. He made each constellation over her head glow brightly and then change into the object it was named for, and he brought the rabbits out of their holes to dance.

Then he showed her goblin magic. He made a fire of rainbow flames. He made a wall of glowing smoke that encircled the two of them in a golden room, and he wrote her name in fiery sparks at her feet.

Jane watched everything in a delight beyond words, her sparkling eyes huge in her pinched face. And when he finally led her back to her house and said good-bye, she threw her arms around his neck and kissed him.

"I'll never forget real magic," she said. "Tonight was a happy ending all its own."

Seylin set off into the woods again, glad to have made her happy, but the shy young man walked all night long, determined to put some distance between himself and the human world that had placed a little claim on his affection. When dawn came, he pitched his tent deep in the forest and slept soundly all day, far from human dwellings.

While he ate his meal in the early twilight that evening, he thought again about Jane. He began to feel anxious. Something hadn't been right. The kiss! Those lips and thin arms had been so hot when they had touched him! They shouldn't have been like that. He remembered Jane's sparkling eyes, her chattering teeth. The little girl had been burning up with fever.

Seylin broke camp as quickly as he could and began to retrace his steps. As he walked, he argued with himself. What did a human mean to elves or goblins? If this neglected girl were to die, that wasn't his fault. She meant nothing to him, nothing at all, and he had given her a pleasant memory to think about while she was dying. What more should elves and goblins do for a human? Humans never did anything for them.

But even as Seylin argued, he walked faster, and he scanned the ground for the herbs used in the Fever Spell. He had very little experience with human illness. Emily had been sick several times, but Marak had cured her as soon as she began to feel bad. Jane's skinny body had been sick now for at least two days. He doubted she would survive without help.

He arrived at the dilapidated house a couple of hours before dawn to find light glimmering from an upstairs window. He changed into a cat and quickly scrambled up a nearby tree. A candle flickered in the little girl's bedroom, and she lay quite still beneath the covers. Her wise and handsome father sat sobbing beside her, her hands clasped in his own.

Seylin lashed his tail furiously. He was too late. This was poor little Jane's happy ending. But just as he was about to climb down from his tree and set out again on his journey, he saw her twitch beneath the covers. She wasn't dead yet.

The reserved young man who had been raised never to interfere with humans didn't hesitate for a second. He was out of the tree in two bounds. He changed into his own form, retrieved his fever herbs, and was in the house and up the stairs as fast as he could move. Jane's father reeled back at the sight of him, but Seylin didn't stop for introductions.

"Bring me a cup of boiling water," he ordered.

A kettle was already on the grate, so his hot water arrived quickly. The young man set it carefully on the floor and put the herbs into it, whispering the spell over the dirty cup.

"Jane," he said when it was ready, putting his hand on that blazing forehead; but, just like the elf girl in his story, Jane didn't know he was there. He turned to her father, who was watching him with hollow eyes.

"I need a spoon," he said. "Help me get this into her." They managed to spoon the hot liquid into the girl's mouth, and by the time it was half gone, she was able to drink it from the cup.

So much for the fever, thought the pleased Seylin, and he began to murmur the Locating Spell. He expected to find her lungs damaged, or her head, or her stomach. Instead, he found damage over her entire body. There it was, the disease that held her, a bright red rash at the moment. It was very common in the human world, and when it didn't kill, it scarred for life. The goblins had no spell to treat this disease; their human brides were safe from it in the underground kingdom. The nomadic elves had no such protected climate for the elf King's human wife or the human slaves they sometimes used. They had a spell for it, but what was it? Which constellation? Seylin closed his eyes, thinking hard.

That was it. He had it now. It centered on the moon, with its scars and circles. In his mind, he reached for the crescent moon and repeated the words of the spell. The bright red rash faded away before his eyes, leaving the skin pale and smooth.

"Do you know you're in danger?" stammered the unkempt man. "My daughter has smallpox."

"No, she doesn't," answered Seylin in relief. Jane was free of illness. But she was still underfed, neglected, dirty, lonely, unhealthy, and unhappy. He was already interfering in the human world. Why stop now?

"It's a miracle!" the man breathed. "A miracle! I saw it!"

"No," answered Seylin. "It's not a real miracle, just a happy ending caused by magic worked by an elf raised by goblins. You didn't tell your daughter the truth. You filled her head with stories and then took them away from her. And she adores you; she thinks her wise and handsome father knows everything. If I had a daughter like this, I'd give her more to live on than lies. Regular meals would be a good start."

The man sank down on the foot of the bed.

"You don't understand," he replied. "I grew up a gentleman. I'm not prepared for this kind of life. My mother wanted me to make a name for myself in politics, but I came home from college, and that's when I met Liza."

"Is that the beautiful maiden your daughter talked about?" asked Seylin. "Why were you forbidden to speak to her?"

The man gave a rueful shrug. "Is a gentleman ever supposed to converse with the housemaids? But she was right about Liza's beauty. I was wild about the girl. I won her trust, and I ruined her. When my mother found out she was pregnant, she dismissed her from service. Nobody would give her any work.

"There was my poor Liza, out in the street, and my child with her. I decided to marry her. But my mother was so angry when she learned of the marriage that she threw me out, too, and now Liza and I were in the street together. I had never learned how to make a living, so Liza worked for us both. She died soon after Jane's birth. I make a little money every now and then, when I can find something to do. Really, I don't know how. It's just not something I was taught."

Seylin surveyed the human with growing disgust. "You'd have more money for food if you didn't drink away what you get, and you'd earn more money if you weren't still drunk in the mornings. Jane loves magic. She'll be thrilled to find out that her father is under an enchantment." He concentrated for a minute and tapped the human on the shoulder. Then he picked up his herbs and walked to the door.

"Wait a minute!" said the man, upset. "What did you just do?"

"That's an elf spell," Seylin told him, "to keep the human slaves out of the winter cider. Try drinking anything but water now and you'll just throw it up. That should help you wake up in the morning."

He walked outside to retrieve his dewy pack. The sky was brightening in the east, but he still had some time left. Seylin set out at a steady pace. He would be miles away from this depressing house before the day broke in earnest.

Chapter Four

"They're eating me alive!" shrieked Emily, and she dropped the pack to scratch. She was standing on a hedge-lined road that ran between flat fields, water-logged and muddy with recent rainfall. Midges and gnats whined past her ears and danced before her eyes.

The scrawny gray squirrel on her shoulder clung tightly to its perch and chattered with disapproval. "I never heard such a fuss over a few tiny bugs!" it shrilled. "All this hysterical skipping about! Your sister would never do anything so undignified."

Kate and Ruby had had only one unfriendly encounter, and that had happened before Kate became Marak's wife. Changed into a squirrel, Ruby had taken a turn at guarding the King's Bride from harm, and the furious Kate had chased her up a tree. But all was forgiven after the ceremony. Kate could do no wrong. After all, as Ruby often remarked in reverent tones, the King's Wife was an elf.

"Oh, I am just so *sick* of hearing you talk about my sister!" cried Emily. "She had the same mother and father that I had! How can she be an elf and be *perfect,* and I'm just a horrid human? Well? Answer me that!"

"It's a dreadful misfortune," agreed the squirrel. "For all of us," it added quietly.

"And how is it that you're supposed to be protecting me and you're letting these things bite me by the dozen? I can't wait to tell Marak how you've failed his trust."

"The King stressed that you were to experience your world just like a regular human. Bugs belong to your world, and you're experiencing them," Ruby replied with evident satisfaction.

"I'll tell Marak that you let me be attacked by wild beasts," threatened Emily.

"A midge is hardly a wild beast."

"Then tame one!"

The squirrel chattered and grumbled for a few seconds. "All right. Goodness! Such a commotion over a few bites." And she worked the Insect Spell. Silence reigned for a quarter of an hour as Emily squelched down the muddy road.

"Now it's starting to rain again! Ruby, why won't you work the Rain Spell? I'm already soaked to the skin."

"I am not allowed to interfere unless you are in danger. Comfort," enunciated her former teacher, "does not belong to the human world."

"Neither do talking squirrels," said Emily viciously.

"I've had enough," snapped the squirrel. "I'm going to find some peace and quiet. Scream if you really need my help, and I'll come save you." She bounded from Emily's shoulder down to the road, ran lightly across the top of the mud, and disappeared through a hole in the hedge.

Emily picked her way along, studying the dark clouds overhead and trying to keep up her spirits. They could hardly be lower. Except for his one trading journey, she and Seylin had never been apart for any length of time. She remembered how miserable she had been while he was gone. All the diversions of the goblin kingdom hadn't been enough to replace him. He had come back stiff and formal, and she had been angry about it, but she had still seen his embarrassed face at least once a day. She had assumed that she always would.

Now she hadn't seen him in weeks, and she missed him dreadfully, more than she had ever missed anyone. She had to find him again. She couldn't imagine life without him. In her mind, she practiced the speech she would say when they met. It had changed over the course of the last few weeks. "Get married? I don't really want to marry any-body, but if I have to, I'll marry you." "Get married? If you feel that way, it's all right with me." "Get married? I'd like to—if it's with you, I mean." And now, "Where are you, for heaven's sake? Why aren't you looking for me? Seylin, don't you want to get married?"

Loud barking interrupted her reverie. The gray squirrel came flying across the road and charged up her, clambering onto the top of the pack. A couple of mongrels, baying noisily, burst through a gap in the hedge. Two small boys followed them, waving sticks and yelling.

"Hey, she's got our squirrel!"

"Give it back, then!"

Emily put a hand over the trembling creature and kicked the nearest of the dogs. "It's mine now," she announced firmly. "You can't have it."

The larger boy pushed his cap from his forehead and studied the squirrel critically.

"Ah, come on, Archie," he said to his companion. "It's ratty-looking, anyway."

In another minute, they were out of sight, and Ruby was her accustomed form. Breathing heavily, the woman pulled her hood low over her eyes and sat down upon the step of a nearby stile.

"Why did you let them chase you?" demanded Emily in amuse-ment. "You had all sorts of magic you could work."

"I—I don't know," panted Ruby. "They just looked so big, and"—she wiped her brow—"I think I just panicked."

Emily was moved to grudging sympathy. "It could have hap-pened to anybody, I suppose," she observed, taking out their water flask and handing it over. "Why don't you stay here and rest. There's a village just down the road, in that clump of trees. I'll go find some shelter."

"You'll go ask after Seylin."

The young woman put down her pack and stared. She was completely thunderstruck. During the whole boring, difficult journey, she hadn't mentioned Seylin once.

"What did Marak tell you?" she demanded indignantly.

"What would the King need to tell me?" Ruby took a drink. "Before breakfast, he told me that you were leaving on some ridiculous quest. During breakfast, he told us all that Seylin had just left on a serious one. You always did keep that boy's heart on a string, and you're furious that he's decided to find an elf."

Emily was outraged.

"I never kept his heart anywhere, and he didn't decide to find an elf! If you want to know the truth, he asked to marry me."

"And why didn't he?"

"There was a misunderstanding."

Ruby glared at her from beneath the hood. "I feel sure of that! Then you shot out of the kingdom like an arrow from a bow, without even stopping to think. You walked right past Seylin's tracks four different times and didn't even notice. You're dragging me all over this dismal countryside without a hope of finding him. Isn't that just like a human!"

She climbed to her feet and began walking down the road, shading her eyes on that dark, stormy day from what little sunlight there was.

Emily opened her mouth to say something scathing, but she didn't. Instead, she thought carefully for a minute and arranged her features into a humble expression.

"If only I knew what I was doing wrong," she mourned.

"You're not thinking like an elf," declared the teacher triumphantly. "You're asking every human you meet about Seylin when you think I'm not nearby. Humans won't see Seylin. Humans never did see the elves. You won't learn anything that way."

"You would know where to look for him," Emily said softly, looking so humble that she thought her face would crack. "You wouldn't make the mistakes I'm making. You'd know how to think like an elf."

It worked. Ruby's voice grew distant and thoughtful.

"Yes, I would," she replied. "If I were looking for Seylin, I'd be in the elf King's forest."

"The forest?" Emily was disappointed. "We looked there, and I didn't find a thing."

"Oh, no, we didn't. You just looked in the small strip of woodland that lies on goblin land. The elf King's forest is huge. No one goes there now. Humans are afraid of it because the elf spells still linger. Goblins don't like it, either, but I'd like to walk through it just once."

"Really?" Emily was interested in spite of herself. "Why would you, if goblins don't like it?"

"Because I'm a strong elf cross," replied Ruby smugly. "That's where I got my hair."

"Oh," remarked Emily. She couldn't think of anything more complimentary to say. "Then we'll go there, Ruby. I think you're right. We'll look for Seylin the elf way."

Ruby crossed her arms. "I'm not helping you find him," she declared.

Emily grinned. "I think you already have."

⌒

In the goblin kingdom, the little children had stopped asking when Emily would come back. They walked sadly by their playmate's empty apartment and wondered where she was. Catspaw and Til in particular were hard-hit by the loss. The human orphan that Kate had saved from the sorcerer's lair and her foster brother, the goblin prince, both adored their aunt Emily. She was the only person in the kingdom who could distract the two children so well that they forgot to quarrel with each other.

The nurse brought the children into the royal rooms for the walk down to the banquet hall. Kate and Marak heard them coming well before they saw them.

"Father!"

"Papa!"

The pair charged in, racing to be the first to reach Marak. Til was older and larger and took the lead for an easy win, but the young prince stretched out his lion's paw after her as she ran by. She began to slide backward with every step, running as hard as she could and going nowhere. But as Catspaw trotted past the angry girl, she socked him hard in the stomach. Catspaw doubled over, and Til won the race.

"Papa, Papa!" she cried, clambering onto his lap. The goblin King put one arm around her and held the other out toward his angry son.

"No vengeful magic!" he ordered sharply, intercepting the bolt, and whatever Catspaw had intended for Til didn't happen. He had to fall back instead on that childhood favorite, the verbal insult.

"You don't have a Father!" He scowled, walking up to his father, whose lap was now full.

"You don't have a Papa," retorted the little girl, leering at him from her prized vantage point.

"Silence," commanded the goblin King, catching his son's paw to prevent further outbursts. "Til, you just struck Catspaw. You know that's wrong, and it's also very dangerous. What do you have to say about it?"

Til's mobile young face crumpled at once, and her black eyes filled with tears. "But he's so mean, Papa," she quavered. "I hate Catspaw! He's always doing things like that to me."

"So he is," commented Marak, patting her short black hair, which Catspaw had only recently singed off again. "Since you hate Catspaw, you'll be glad to know that I have some new playmates for you. Tomorrow you can come with your mother and me to the pages' floor to see your room, and you and another little girl will stay in that room and be pages together."

"I don't want to stay with another little girl," she whimpered. "I hate little girls!"

"Til," said the goblin dryly, "you're a little girl yourself." Til stopped crying to think about this.

"Father?" asked Catspaw anxiously. "Can I be a pages-together, too?" Marak pulled on the little lion's paw and drew his son close.

"No, you won't be a page, but you'll have a tutor soon," he promised, putting an arm around him. "You have to start learning how to be a King."

Til saw an immediate advantage to her new social position. "You don't get to be a page," she gloated to the little prince. "*I* get to be a page."

Catspaw rallied at once. "You don't get to be a King," he retorted.

"I don't want to," sniffed Til. "They don't let Kings have any fun."

"Oh, I don't know about that," chuckled Marak, pushing her off his lap and standing up. "Come along now, Til. You can meet that little girl you hate."

Til inspired the pages with awe, and she pointed out at every oppor-tunity to Catspaw that she had now outgrown his company. Catspaw was jealous over Til's new career and too young to under-stand why his aunt Emily had left. Everything was changing around the goblin prince, but he was still doing the same things.

One day, he stayed with Agatha while his mother taught class. Marak's former nurse had finally given up keeping order on the pages' floor. She was too old to chase after a crowd of children. Catspaw was unhappy and out of sorts, and Agatha was no help. Usually the dwarf woman was lively and full of fun, but today he could hardly get her to move. She watched him throwing his ball and retrieving it with a stern look on her face.

"Stop making so much noise, Marak," she commanded. Agatha was the only person in the kingdom who called the prince by his formal name. "You tell your father that you're old enough to have a tutor now."

This interested Catspaw. He rolled the ball to her feet and followed it.

"Father says soon," he told her seriously. "I'll learn magic and history and writing and cooking and all sorts of king stuff."

Agatha leaned her head back on her chair. "Kings don't learn how to cook," she said wearily.

"Why not?" asked Catspaw, bouncing the ball around her chair. He was making her head hurt.

"Marak, tell your father you need a tutor," she repeated firmly. "Your nurse is tired."

"Nana's not tired," he said, thinking of his woolly nurse. Nana knew he missed Til. She had had a pillow fight with him just that morning.

"Your nurse is tired," said Agatha, closing her eyes. "Come here, young Marak. It's time for your nap."

Catspaw stopped and goggled at her. He was too old for naps. No worse injustice can be perpetrated on a child than to force a nap on him after he has grown out of them.

"Agatha!" he shrilled reproachfully. "I don't take naps."

The dwarf woman opened her eyes again. They snapped at him commandingly. Catspaw had known that she'd been Father's nurse, and he'd always wondered how such a little woman could make such a big man behave. Now he understood.

"Marak, come here," she ordered him sharply, and Catspaw put down his ball and came. "Climb up, then," she said, pulling him into her arms. The young prince sat in the dwarf woman's lap and looked at her. He twined his arms around her neck. It finally dawned on him that she was the one who was tired. This struck him as a huge joke.

"You're not my nurse, Agatha." He giggled. "Nana's my nurse."

Those eyes snapped and sparkled at him fiercely. "I have always been your nurse, Marak!" Then she softened at the hurt look on his face.

"Now, dear, take your nap," she muttered, tucking his head onto her shoulder and his legs across her lap. Catspaw blinked at the side of her face in surprise. He didn't know what to do. But there *was* nothing to do. Til wouldn't play with him anymore, and his aunt Emily was gone. He closed his eyes. Agatha held him and looked off into the distance, feeling him relax into sleep. Then she closed her own eyes with a sigh.

And that is how the goblin King found them when he came to fetch his son, the young and the old nestled together in each other's arms. Marak knelt by the chair for a long time, just looking at them. They were resting so quietly, their faces so peaceful. But only one of them was asleep.

Chapter Five

"It's such a creepy place," remarked Emily, peering up at the tall trees. "I never knew that a lovely thing could be frightening."

"It's full of memories." The squirrel on her shoulder gave a tiny sigh. "Some of them are unhappy ones."

The forest was very, very old. Many of the trees were mossy and enormous. But, unlike a regular forest, this place had no broken, rotting trunks, fallen limbs, or blasted branches. Autumn had come, and trees unknown to Emily were covered with red and gold leaves, but a carpet of green turf and bracken covered the ground, and tiny flowers nodded at their feet. Birds sang quietly in the distance.

"It isn't natural," said Emily suspiciously. "A forest can't look like this."

"The elves built this forest, just as the dwarves built the goblin caves," lectured the squirrel. "They made it as beautiful as they were. They worked with living things, not stone or brick, and their tools were spells. Many of those spells still hold force."

"Where are the spells against us?" muttered Emily. The place didn't feel friendly.

"The Border Spell used to keep your people out entirely, and only a handful of the most powerful goblins could get through. They crossed the border one at a time, vulnerable to patrolling elves. But that spell was the first thing to go, even before the last elf King's death."

Day after day, Emily walked through the glorious wood, wading through clear streams and crossing short-cropped meadows. Ruby called these dancing fields. Deer grazed there even in the full light of day.

Once, the young woman stopped short in surprise. "I thought I saw a sheep," she said. "It ran between those trees."

"Sheep have always lived in these woods," replied the teacher, and Emily didn't ask why.

One afternoon, they came to a deep fold in the hills. The trees in this narrow valley were widely spaced and colossal. One great pine towered two hundred feet into the air. It stood in a half-circle of old holly trees.

"Em!" For once, the annoying squirrel's voice was hushed and gentle. "Look at that! We've found the elf King's winter camp. He used to hold court under that pine, and all the lords and ladies of the King's Camp danced on the smooth lawn below it."

They stopped to have lunch, but neither could eat. The beautiful valley lay dreaming under a spell of its own. Without meaning to, they lingered. Emily napped, and the squirrel climbed to the very top of the huge pine. As twilight fell, Emily strolled about, investigating, while Ruby changed back into her regular form and sat under the holly trees, thinking her own thoughts.

"I've found something!" Emily hurried through the trees. "Bones! They've been here a long time."

Ruby came with her and knelt down by the bones. They were white and delicate, half buried under moss. "It must be a child, the skull is so small." The goblin woman looked around. "Probably it was wounded, and it dragged itself into the shelter of the trees to hide. No one found it, poor thing."

"Hide?" Emily was puzzled. Ruby gave her an irritated look.

"You never did pay attention to your lessons," she declared.

"Don't you remember anything? This was the scene of the last battle of the elf harrowing!"

"Oh," breathed the young woman. "I knew that. I just forgot. And it doesn't look much like a battlefield, does it?"

"How should a battlefield look after two hundred years?" demanded Ruby. She walked away from the graceful skeleton. Emily followed her, studying the charming scenery with new eyes. After the death of the last elf King, the goblins had waged war to capture all the elf brides they could. They called this war of plunder the elf harrowing.

"How did the battle take place?" she wanted to know. "Was it quick? Did many people die?"

"Lore-Master Webfoot probably asked you the same questions. Did you earn a perfect score on his tests?" But Emily knew when to keep silent, and the born teacher couldn't resist the chance to teach.

"It was the dead of winter, and bitterly cold," she grudgingly began. "Almost every other elf camp was in ruins by that time, and the King's Camp had lost contact with the survivors. They knew that the goblin King would come to attack the elf King's winter camp, and they knew that their entire race was doomed.

"Even though the elf King was dead, this camp had a formidable guard. The highest lords of the land had always lived in it: the Lords of Counsel, the Lords of Enchantment, the elf King's Scholars, and his military commander. They were an aristocracy of magic, and from the oldest widows down to the small children, they swore to fight to the death. They did, too. Only a few babies survived."

Emily thought about this. It was hard to imagine a small child or an old woman fighting anyone.

"What did they use as weapons?"

"Magic, of course."

"But how? What did the battle look like?"

Ruby considered the question. "It looked terrifying. They said that it was like walking into the middle of a storm cloud. Brilliant flashes of light were everywhere. No one could see. The lords and ladies—even the children—worked a single spell together, so that when one of them fell the rest made up for the loss. As a united force, they were stronger than the goblin King himself, and they killed hundreds of goblins. The King's two lieutenants and most of the King's Guard were among them."

"That means all those elf brides they had captured didn't have husbands anymore."

The ugly woman studied the ground. "I suppose they didn't," she agreed reluctantly.

"But I thought that was the point of the elf harrowing, to take brides. If you ask me, attacking this camp wasn't very smart."

"No one asked you!" Ruby was stung by the criticism. "Marak Whiteye knew exactly what he was doing. He wanted the elf King's library. He packed up the whole set of elvish spell books and chronicles and brought them back to the kingdom. Now we study the elf King's books, and we know how to work their magic."

"That's right!" exclaimed Emily in excitement. "I remember now. The elf King's library was kept in caves because that's where the elves lived during the winter. Those caves must be here somewhere, Ruby. Let's go find them."

Deep twilight had fallen. Ruby lit a flickering orange flame and carried it in the palm of her hand. Emily preferred Seylin's moon globes and said so, but the teacher gave her a nasty look. "If you don't like goblin magic, use some of your own," she said. And that ended the discussion.

They scanned the rocky faces that hemmed in the narrow valley, but they found no cleft or opening. "Think like an elf," mused Ruby. "They must have disguised it, but with what?"

"With living things," suggested Emily, and that turned out to be the case. A thick mat of vines hung down over one low cliff. Ruby brushed them aside and discovered that a narrow gap lay beyond. In another minute, they were inside a cave that could have held a crowd of hundreds.

"This is the largest cave I've ever seen," breathed Emily. Ruby gave a scornful laugh. "I know," amended the young woman hastily, "that the goblin kingdom is much bigger. But the kingdom doesn't look like a real cave."

"This," remarked Ruby, "doesn't look like a real cave, either."

She was right. It looked instead like the center of an enormous geode, with great crystal faces and formations studding the walls and ceiling. The sparkling dome caught the orange goblin light thousands of times, like the quick, winking dance of fireflies. Underfoot lay a coarse silvery sand, firm yet inviting to the foot. The grains of sand spread the light as well, glimmering like tiny diamonds.

"They danced here while the storms howled outside," said the goblin woman sadly.

Emily looked around the splendid room that seemed so natural, yet so magical. She tried to imagine beautiful elves dancing and laughing and leading their carefree lives. The wind-rippled sand showed no tracks of animals or insects, not even the tiniest mouse or spider. Spells still kept this great cave pristine. They walked by a harp lying near the wall, its strings broken and tangled. The curving wooden frame reminded Emily of the bones they had seen. This harp was just as graceful, and just as dead.

"That way lies an underground spring." Ruby gestured toward another narrow opening. "Beyond it are the storerooms and the elf King's library."

"The library? Let's go see what they left behind!" said Emily eagerly, but the goblin woman stiffened.

"Nothing was left behind," she said in her most disapproving classroom voice. "The goblin King himself supervised the removal of the books."

Emily wouldn't be dampened in her treasure-hunting zeal. "They're bound to have forgotten something," she declared. "Remember, they didn't find that child's body. Come on!"

Ruby stopped where she was.

"They weren't hunting for bodies," she said coldly. "The goblin King said that they had found everything they came for, and that is quite enough for me. It ought to be enough for you, but humans don't know the meaning of 'enough.' The impertinence! Thinking that you know better than a King!"

"Do you mean," demanded Emily in complete astonishment, "that you've come to a place like this, and you aren't even going to poke around at *all*? What on earth is the matter with you?"

"That is just what I mean." Ruby glared at her. "And what on earth is the matter with *you*?"

"You goblins are so sanctimonious!"

"You humans are absurd."

"Well, I'm going into those rooms!"

"Then you can go alone."

Emily hesitated. "I need a light," she stated with as much dignity as she could. "I'll go without one if I have to, and I'll fall into that underground spring and drown. But don't worry; I'm sure Marak won't mind."

Ruby grumbled for a few seconds. "Oh, if you must!" she snapped.

A flickering flame appeared right in front of Emily's eyes and defied her efforts to move it. The goblin woman turned on her heel and walked away.

❧

The narrow corridor beyond the cave was quite steep, and a sizable stream rushed down the middle of it, cascading melodiously from waterfall to waterfall. It was a lovely place, or would have been if it weren't quite so dangerous. The watercourse took up almost the whole width of the passage, with the smallest rocky trails on either side. Emily was obliged at times to crawl along the slim ledges on her hands and knees while the spray of the pounding water flew around her and the goblin light made spots before her eyes. This was one place, she thought, where the legendary grace of the elves really would have come in handy.

She came to a big round room. In the center stood a large hexagonal piece of furniture carved from the native rock. A six-sided pyramid formed its core, raised on a slender column about three feet from the floor of the cave and surrounded by a hexagonal ring of stone benches. Emily walked around it, wondering what it was for. Only when she sat down on one of the benches and turned to face the center did she understand. Each face of the pyramid formed a triangular writing desk, angled to bring the pages of a book comfortably close to the reader. A lip at the bottom kept the book from sliding to the floor. Six scholars could sit around the pyramid and study their books at the same time. This must have been the library!

Emily jumped up and examined the room, her goblin light leading the way. Above the center of the pyramid gleamed a silver globe, but whether it was suspended from the ceiling or simply hung in space, she couldn't determine. A faint light came from it, joining her flame to illuminate six long, narrow fissures that rose in a shallow spiral pattern, circling the walls. Emily puzzled over them, running her finger down the slanting cavity of the nearest one. It could almost be a bookshelf, she decided, carved into the rock, if one didn't mind that the books would not be level. The upper ones would lean against the lower ones, rising in their shallow curve. A scholar would need lots of strength to pull out the books closest to the floor—or the proper magic. But the angled curves of books would appear to float up the walls in a charming dance.

Not so much as a scrap of parchment remained in any of the curving shelves. Emily was disappointed. She supposed that Ruby was right, and why shouldn't she be? The goblin King himself had supervised their removal. Returning to the door, she stumbled over something. A cloth-covered bundle lay under one of the benches. Emily pulled away the bulky cloth and examined her find. It was a leather-bound book.

Wrapping up her discovery, Emily hurried from the room. Once again, she had to creep down the dangerous passage by the cascading waterfall. She tried not to imagine herself swept away by the rushing water and drowned in some subterranean tunnel. Any other race would have cut steps into the rock, but, oh, no, not the elves. Everything had to be perfectly, unnaturally natural.

Ruby had lit their supper fire near the semicircle of holly trees, facing the open vista beyond their narrow valley. Stars were just coming out in the evening sky. Emily walked up slowly, studying her treasure and trailing the heavy cloth. She couldn't speak elvish, but goblins and elves shared a script of magical characters. Most nouns and verbs were represented by a symbol that looked and meant almost the same thing to an elf or a goblin, even though it didn't sound the same in the two different languages.

"What does the character 'ugly' mean to the elves?" she wanted to know. "I'm finding it everywhere."

"That's the elvish word *niddug*. It means 'goblins.' Humph!" snorted Ruby, stirring up the fire. "We have words for them, too." Then she turned around in surprise. "What do you have there?"

"Something the ugly goblins forgot," announced Emily in triumph. "I found an elvish book. Look, it has the symbol for goblins on almost every page," she said, sitting down next to the teacher. "And here, on the first page, is the number four, so it must be a volume of a set."

Ruby examined the pages, dumbfounded.

"Em!" Her voice was a whisper. "You've found Mouse's book! That's her elvish name, Lim, on the first page."

"Mouse? Who's Mouse? Someone named Four? I'd hate to have a name like that."

"She was the fourth baby. It's so rare for an elf woman to have that many children that those babies are always named Four. But the goblins never called her that. Marak Blackwing nicknamed her Mouse, and that's what she was for the rest of her life."

"I remember something about her," lied Emily cautiously, but for once Ruby didn't bother to scold her.

"Mouse came to the kingdom to try to free her father, who was in prison for killing goblins. The goblin King offered her the choice of marrying him and saving her father's life, or of going free and causing her father's execution. Mouse lived in the kingdom for three months before she had to make her decision, and she spent the whole time studying goblins. Her elf fiancé was a scholar, and she wanted to be one, too. That's when she wrote this book.

"Marak Blackwing recorded in the chronicles that Mouse never intended to marry him. She always told him that she would go back to her people when the three months were up. The goblin King fell in love with her, and he released her father rather than force her to choose his death. But when he told Mouse that, she decided to marry him after all. He sent her book to the elves with the announcement that she had become the King's Wife."

"Why would she do that?" asked Emily, flipping through the volume. There was a crude sketch of the throne room on one page, and a diagram of a typical palace apartment on another. "Had Mouse fallen in love with Marak Blackwing, too?"

"Goodness, no," answered the goblin woman sincerely. "Not for a long time. Mouse was a strong, brave woman, and she realized her elf King was a fool. Mouse knew that her people couldn't protect themselves, so she stayed to be a friend of the elves in the goblin King's court. Her plan worked. Marak Blackwing adored her, and he would have given her anything. He never harmed another elf as long as he lived. Their son, Marak Whiteye, actually protected the elves until the death of their last King. Then, of course, there was nothing he could do for them."

"Wait a minute!" interrupted Emily. "Do you mean that the son of this amazing elf was the goblin King who ordered the elf harrowing? The goblin King who destroyed this very camp? Some friend of the elves he was!"

"I said there was nothing he could do," snapped Ruby. "The elves couldn't survive without their King. They must have hidden his mother's book because they knew he wanted it so much. That's a nice dose of elvish spite for you."

"They didn't hide it at all," argued Emily. "I practically fell over it."

"Don't be ridiculous! It must have been hidden by a spell, and the spell wore off over the years."

"It was wrapped in this," explained Emily, standing up and dragging the heavy folds forward. Ruby stood up to take them from her. Then she sat down with a jolt.

"No," she gasped. "No! It can't be!"

"What is it?" demanded Emily, pulling back the folds to shake them out. They formed a perfectly ordinary cloak, undamaged by time. A black cloak, of the sort that the King's Guard always wore.

"A goblin hid it?" she asked slowly, turning it in her hands. "The book that the goblin King wanted? I don't see how that's possible!"

Ruby didn't explain. She sat without speaking, rocking back and forth, obviously quite distraught.

Their supper was ready, but Ruby didn't eat. Emily ate heartily, meanwhile making plans. The old goblin woman didn't want to tell her what was wrong, but getting things out of people who didn't want to give them was one of Emily's specialties.

"Mouse must have been an outstanding King's Wife," she remarked in a casual tone. "Her son must have been a great goblin King."

"He should have been." Ruby's voice was unsteady. "He had tremendous gifts. He spoke and read elvish like one of their own scholars, and he knew more of their history than their own lords did. He dressed like an elf and hunted like an elf. He even looked like an elf."

"He did? The goblin King?" Emily thought of Seylin and all the teasing he had endured. She supposed a goblin King could be teased, too, but it was hard to imagine.

"Well, he did have blue skin and white hair," amended Ruby, "and white eyes like mine. But aside from that, he looked just like an elf. Marak Whiteye put his own Guard to watch the elf King's borders when he discovered that the Border Spell was gone. And when he heard of the death of the elf King, he realized his destiny. He was to be the first King of the two races."

"How did he get from that destiny to butchering them all?" Emily demanded. Ruby turned evasive.

"It was their fault, really," she muttered. "The elf lords insulted him. And when he pointed out that his mother had sacrificed her life for those worthless lords, they insulted his mother, too. They said that she had done nothing for the elves: she had produced another goblin. As far as they were concerned, she had wasted her whole life."

"So Marak Whiteye took revenge," said Emily with growing comprehension. "He took goblin revenge for his mother's sake, and he proved the elf lords right."

"He swore to kill as many elf men as he could." Ruby sighed. "And he wasn't particular about the women and children who got killed, either. His mother was dead herself by that time. There was no one to talk him out of it. He wanted their books of magic for himself, and he was determined to have this book, too. It held a secret. Mouse had written in it all day before she decided to become the King's Wife. But she couldn't remember what she had written, and her husband never would tell her."

"This is Whiteye's cloak, isn't it?" asked Emily. "He found his mother's book."

The teacher nodded. "Yes, there are leather ties. Whiteye's cloak was just like an elf cloak, with no metal clasp. He hurt the dwarves' feelings badly. But this isn't a real elf cloak. They never wear black cloth."

"What did his mother write on that last day?" wondered Emily.

They looked at the pages together. The handwriting was hurried and sloppy, almost unreadable in places. Lines broke off in the middle, and characters were scratched out.

"She's written down everything she loves about being an elf," whispered Ruby. "Everything that she's about to lose forever. Her favorite flowers. All the kinds of trees. Dances, friends, foods. The best hills to climb. And here, on the final page, her elvish fiancé's name. 'Please understand,' she writes to him. That's the last thing in the book."

Emily felt a lump in her throat. She imagined the young elf woman saying good-bye to the man she loved, about to condemn herself to a living nightmare.

"Poor Whiteye," she murmured. "He must have read those pages and finally understood that he had destroyed everything his mother loved. He couldn't face the shame of taking the book home. He had to leave it behind."

"He stopped the elf harrowing that night," said Ruby. "The goblins never came back to the elf lands, and Whiteye died bitter and unhappy. Scholars thought that it was grief over the loss of his Guard, but it must have been regret."

"And his mother had had such hopes for him, too," mused Emily. "I wonder what hopes my parents had for me."

"I can tell you what I hope," said the teacher, closing the old book. "You should give up this nonsensical quest and go back to the kingdom to get married."

"I want to marry Seylin," protested Emily. "I can't just give up what I want. You can't ask me to do that. It isn't fair."

But her sister had done it. She had given up everything she loved to save Emily's life. Emily paused, struck for the first time by the courage of Kate's sacrifice. Ruby broke in on her thoughts.

"I can ask you to do it because I've done it myself," she said crisply. "I never wanted to teach about humans; I wanted to teach about the elves. I studied and studied to become an elf lore-master, but Master Webfoot got that subject instead. The King asked me to be the human lore-master, and I did it even though I didn't want to."

"Well, I don't think you should have," declared her former pupil with devastating candor. "You hate the subject, and you make your students hate it, too. Kate gave up what she wanted, but she didn't hate Marak for it. She knew it wouldn't be right."

"I teach my subject as well as I know how!" exclaimed Ruby, deeply offended. "I work harder than anybody else, and my students learn more."

Yesterday, Emily would have argued this point, but today she was silent. What did her family want for her future? What should she do with her life? She had never thought about it in those terms before. She had always considered only what *she* wanted and how to win everyone to her plans. She thought of Kate's frustration and embarrassment over her many escapades. She thought of Marak's endless patience. What did he hope for her?

"Why do you think Marak sent us out together?" she asked.

"Goblin revenge, obviously," snapped the old teacher. "Though for the life of me I can't recall what I did to deserve it."

"I deserve it," admitted Emily promptly. "But I don't think that's the answer. Marak wants something for us both out here. There are things that he wants us to find."

She studied Ruby's ugly features in the flickering firelight as if she were seeing them for the first time. It had never occurred to her before that the teacher might have problems of her own. "Ruby, have you ever tried to understand the human race? Actually tried to like your subject?"

"Who could do that?" Ruby muttered, but her voice lacked its usual sting.

"Humans aren't the only ones who are ruthless and irrational. This battle"—Emily gestured around them—"is as nasty as anything from my world. Have you ever tried to admire us? Have you ever looked at what we've achieved?"

"I've seen Hallow Hill," said the goblin with a sniff. "The dwarves could have built it in their sleep."

"I don't know what Marak wants for me out here," reflected Emily, "but I do have an idea what he wants for you. We'll stop looking for Seylin for a while. I'm going to take you to London. There's bound to be something in that hodgepodge of a place to impress you."

chapter Six

Seylin roamed about the countryside throughout the autumn, traveling back and forth across the harvested fields. After the last elf King's death, goblin scholars had conjectured that the rest of the elves would die off within two or three generations. Then the elf harrowing had taken place. No more vicious war had been waged by the goblins in all the previous millennia. As Seylin went farther and farther without finding a single hopeful clue, he began to believe that the scholars had been right. The elves must all be gone.

The path of the unhappy young man began to look rather peculiar on the map Marak had hung in his workroom. It was more like a spider's web than a logical journey. Seylin consulted his own map one night in a fit of depression and found the most isolated spot on it, the spot where the villages were farthest apart and where no roads came. That remote spot became his goal.

The terrain was rough. Trees didn't grow here; stones and crags seemed to grow instead. But Seylin attained his lonely goal at last. Almost buried in the cleft of a narrow gorge, a band of tall, thin alder trees stood around a gushing rivulet, and there, in the heart of this tiny patch of sheltered woodland, Seylin found something unexpected and quite wonderful. It wasn't elves, but it was almost as rare.

The rivulet arose as a bubbling spring from a fissure in the wall of the gorge and ran down to its little streambed through an ancient channel. Next to this little spring stood the smallest and oldest of chapels. Seylin had passed the lovely ruins of several great abbeys, their graceful arches rising straight from the green turf beneath and their soaring walls roofed by nothing besides the night sky with its countless sparkling stars. He saw, too, the churches in the towns he passed, with their plain glass windows and battered façades altered to suit a reckless nation declaring its rupture from the mother church.

But this tiny chapel showed no such harsh treatment. The wooden door stood open, nor did it look as if it would easily close again, and only ten people could have worshipped there at once, but Seylin was thrilled to see the old stained-glass windows still intact. He studied the windows in the meager starlight that fell through the bare trees and resolved to come again the next morning, when he could admire their patterns in the daylight.

As he explored the walled valley, Seylin marveled at his find and wondered how these three little windows had come to survive when so much more impressive glass had not. In fact, this glass had had good guardians: the rugged stone hills and the rugged people who lived upon them.

The tiny shrine had stood there since time immemorial, the site of the hermit's hut belonging to an ancient Celtic saint. When armed troops began to rove across the land, enforcing the enthusiasm of their newborn faith upon any monument they met, the quiet inhabi-tants of these hills decided that they did not wish to lose their shrine. It belonged to them just as the great rocks did, as the wide sky and the gentle sheep did. And, rather than lose the graceful statues or the vibrant stained-glass windows, they chipped away the rocky path that led to the gorge instead. As time went on, the people kept their secret even from themselves, the father from his son and the mother from her daughter, until the children aged and gained a certain mod-eration, and it seemed prudent to tell them the old story. So, after cen-turies of destruction and realignment, this tiny chapel still stood while many enormous churches lay in ruins.

The next morning, Seylin came padding back in cat form and

entered the little chapel, his gaze fixed on the vivid round window above the stone altar. If his gaze had been fixed on anything lower, he might have noticed the newly swept floor, and then he wouldn't have been taken by surprise.

"Begone, Satan!" declared a firm voice behind him.

Seylin whirled, his fur on end, to find something else as rare as elves in that day and time. A robust, wrinkled, white-haired priest stood right inside the door, his gray eyes flashing a stern warning. The black cat found it terribly unfair to have to share this beautiful spot with a human, and, even more, with a human who had caught him completely off guard.

"I am not Satan!" he piped indignantly in his shrill cat's voice.

The priest didn't flinch when he spoke, any more than little Jane had done. Both of these unusual humans held world-views more generous than the normal, in which talking cats were not at all impossible.

"Then, whichever of the devilish imps you are, begone anyway," ordered the priest. He was quite as sturdy in his own way as the little chapel, having traveled widely in his youth. He lived there now in a life-style very similar to that of the Celtic saint who had been there before him.

"But I'm not a devilish imp," insisted Seylin. The shy cat probably wouldn't have lingered so long, but the priest who intended to expel him was in fact blocking his path to the door. "I just wanted to enjoy the glass windows. They look so pretty with the light coming through them."

For answer, the priest reached into his pocket for his rosary beads and brandished the crucifix at the bewildered cat. Seylin stepped a little nearer to study the tiny figure, hoping to appear polite.

"It's very nice," he said respectfully, unsure how one should compliment a crucifix. "Not as detailed as the one up there, though," and he waved a paw toward the altar. "I rather like that one better, don't you?"

The priest sat down on the last short bench and viewed the large cat disgustedly.

"You should be ashamed of yourself," he declared. "You know you have no business in a church."

"That's true," agreed Seylin, somewhat abashed, "but I didn't think anyone would mind. I'm not keeping a big crowd of humans out of this one."

"Well, that's a good point," sighed the old priest. "I shouldn't complain. At least someone wants to be here."

He fell into his own thoughts, fingering his beads, while Seylin studied his windows in peace. They depicted the life of the hermit and the spring, along with several miracles belonging to both. The lonely cat plucked up courage to ask the human what the scenes depicted, and the lonely priest actually told the devil cat what he knew. Each enjoyed the other's company, although both reserved men were ashamed about it. As a rule, Seylin didn't approve of humans, and the priest certainly didn't approve of demonic beasts.

"It seems very sad," piped the black cat at the end of the old priest's lecture. "It isn't fair that humans are God's favorites. They don't seem to care one way or the other. I'm sure we would care if all of that magic was done for us."

The priest's gray eyes flashed again.

"You devils had your chance," he said sternly.

"I am not a devil!" shrilled Seylin. "We know about the devils, but we don't have anything to do with them."

"That's likely!" remarked the priest severely. "And what are you if you don't have anything to do with devils?"

"I'm an elf," replied Seylin, rather boldly and incautiously. The priest merely laughed a dry, contemptuous laugh.

"Now, that's a lie, you goblin cat," he declared. Seylin felt deeply hurt. "I know what an elf looks like, and it doesn't look like you."

"You've seen an elf?" mewed Seylin in excitement.

"Yes, I have," asserted the priest with a grave nod. "I've seen two elves," he added grandly.

"But—where? And when?" stammered the flustered cat. The priest's face took on a faraway look.

"When I was younger, newly back from the continent and its troubles, I was traveling not far from the village of Nearing, by a little lake in the wooded hills. As I sat there in the shade of twilight, two elves walked down to the lake. I'll never forget them as long as I live. They were so beautiful and graceful, so splendid and regal. I knew right away they were elves." He came out of his happy reverie and glared accusingly at Seylin. "And they didn't look a thing like you!"

The excited cat stared at the priest, his eyes like lights and his fur all on end. "Thanks!" he squeaked in a hysterical tone, and disappeared in a streak through the door. The old priest felt a little disappointed. There was a story behind the odd behavior of this mysterious cat, and he would have liked very much to know what it was.

Seylin consulted his map. The lake was only a couple of nights' journey from the goblin kingdom, near one border of the elf King's lands. The area was no longer one large forest; instead, small groves grew in the folds of the hills. Seylin had been nearby before, but he had been discouraged by all the human encroachment. Now he hurried back as fast as he could, walking far into dawn and starting as early in the twilight as his eyes would allow. He would have been perfectly happy to walk all day long, but his cat form couldn't shoulder the pack.

He soon found the little lake and the campsite, but it didn't contain quite the evidence of elves that he had expected. The trees that grew there were stately and tall, and the traces of tent sites were in their deepest shade, but here also were the charred remains of a log fire and piles of animal bones. These things certainly didn't belong in a normal elf camp.

Then Seylin found a small elf graveyard, without a single stick or rock to act as a monument. This race never marked the graves of their dead, not even the elf Kings. So elves had been here, and perhaps were still coming, but this was a spring or summer camp, too exposed for cold weather. By now they would be in their winter camp because the first snows had fallen. That meant caves if possible, so Seylin began to travel the limits of the forest in search of them. He meandered back and forth for most of another long, snowy night and found a second little camp. Now he was very excited. One camp might mean humans, but two camps had to mean elves. Only elves moved from place to place in a forest without cutting down the trees.

Just a few more hours till dawn. He paused in a clearing and located the uneven crest of a range of hills in the distance. Perhaps those hills sheltered a modest cave or two. He would try that direction next. Seylin turned to retrieve the pack he had dropped at his feet and stopped, the pack forgotten. A sizzling shock ran through his frame.

Standing in the moonlight was an elf.

For a long moment, the two stood and looked each other over. The elf had thick black hair and green eyes, and his form was lean and muscular. He was wearing brown. Seylin was wearing brown clothes, too because elves always wore brown in the winter. The elf wore a short, belted tunic, and his breeches were gartered below the knees, straps of thin leather crossing in X patterns to hold the cloth close to the calves.

This was the style that elf men had worn for millennia, but the outfit was not of properly made elf cloth. The poorest human farmers had better homespun clothes than this, and Seylin's own garments were luxurious beside it.

"You've been leaving tracks all over the forest," commented the stranger in English. "I've been following you for some time. You walked right by two rabbits just now. What are you hunting for?"

"I'm hunting for you," said Seylin in elvish, but the stranger just looked baffled. "I'm hunting for elves," he added in English. "I thought I might be the last one left."

The other elf considered this. "What happened to the rest of your band?"

Seylin shrugged, uncertain how to respond. "I'm alone now," he answered. The elf looked at his nice clothes, his well-made boots, and his sturdy and capacious pack.

"Your women are all dead, aren't they?" he remarked in a knowing tone. "Thorn will want to see you. Wait here. I'll come back. Don't try to follow me because I'll know, and I don't leave tracks everywhere like you do."

Seylin sat down by his pack and waited, mulling over how to proceed. He had read about elves and daydreamed about elves, but he had never really thought about what would happen if he found any. He supposed he had always expected some wise, fatherly elf to walk up and say, "Seylin! Home at last! You're one of us now!" But it was beginning to look as if that wouldn't happen.

The stranger returned with two more elf men, and they studied Seylin. One of them was still just an adolescent, perhaps fourteen years old. The other didn't look terribly old, either, but there was such a hard, capable look on his face that Seylin felt like an overfed baby. He was very handsome, with blond hair and gray eyes, but his crudely woven clothes were a mass of stains and patches.

"Rowan tells me you're supposed to be the last elf of your band," he said, and his face told Seylin that he didn't believe it. "Your women are dead, aren't they? You'll find no luck here. We only have one girl ourselves. We don't intend to marry her to an outsider, so you might as well keep looking."

Seylin felt his face grow hot.

"I'm not looking for a wife," he protested. "I'm just looking for elves, for a band to join."

"Can you hunt?" the blond man wanted to know, and Seylin nodded. "Then show us. Bring some game back to this spot tonight and you can join our band."

Seylin walked away, trying not to show the dismay that he felt. He hadn't exactly lied. He could hunt; he had just never done very much of it, and what he had done was from horseback. The goblin King had learned from his mother, Adele, a certain reckless enthusiasm for foxhunting, although he never actually let a fox be killed. He put a magical blue stripe on the animal to show that they had caught it, leaving some of the local foxes with five or six stripes apiece. But Seylin doubted very much whether these ragged elves would be impressed by a blue-striped fox. Hunting was literally their survival.

In the chronicles, the elves hunted nothing but deer, and Seylin knew very little about how they did it. After searching fruitlessly for as long as he dared, he decided to attempt a calling spell. Making dinner walk right up to him seemed disgusting, but the mutton that he ate walked right up the lake valley to the slaughterhouse in the palace town.

He paused in a clearing and said what he thought were the right words. Time passed, and his heart sank. He must have botched the spell. Why had he charged out of the kingdom without bothering to learn basic elvish spells? All the fancy magic he knew couldn't make up for the ordinary elf spells he didn't know. Just as he was about to give up, moonlight reflected in large brown eyes. A small doe stepped cautiously out of the forest.

Now Seylin felt sick. He knew that elves ate does, but he had never killed or eaten a female animal in his whole life. This doe was a mother, a sacred thing, and a goblin would rather starve than eat her. He called her up to him and stroked her thin flanks. A mother carrying young. Seylin was sure he couldn't possibly kill her.

With his arm around the doe's neck, he said the spell again, and the two of them waited and waited. Just when he was wondering if he really could bring himself to kill her, he saw movement in the trees again. Seylin reached quickly toward the new deer, light blaz-ing from his fingertips. The startled doe leapt away from him and bounded off into the forest.

Seylin examined his kill. A handsome stag of some winters lay at his feet. He took a firm hold on the stag's ear and whispered the elvish Carrying Spell. He guided the body off the ground to a height of a couple of feet and towed it behind him as he walked along, the stag slipping through the forest on a cushion of air.

The blond-haired elf and the adolescent were waiting where he had left them. When Seylin walked up with nothing in his hands, the youngster grinned and pointed.

"See?" he said triumphantly. The elf leader looked disgusted.

"Well? Where's the food?" he demanded.

Seylin gestured behind him.

"I didn't have anyone to help carry it," he said, pulling on the ear and bringing the stag into view.

The pair gawked at the dark body gliding above the snow. The leader recovered first.

"See?" he retorted to the boy. "And he doesn't even know this for-est. I don't want to hear any more of your excuses." He clapped the successful hunter warmly on the shoulder. "What's your name?" he asked.

"Seylin," replied Seylin, stiff with apprehension. He probably should have chosen an elvish name.

"Seylin?" hooted the teenage elf. "What kind of name is that?" It was goblin, of course. Would he have to lie about it?

"Shut up, Willow," ordered the elf man, and the subject was closed. "Seylin, my name is Thorn, and I lead this camp. You can stay if you want to hunt for your share and if you remember what I said about the girl."

Seylin nodded silently. He followed the two men through the woods, trying to sort out his feelings.

They arrived at the winter camp. A hovel of sorts had been constructed by walling up a cave with boards, and a dilapidated shed stood nearby. Seylin lowered the stag to the ground and eased his pack from his shoulders, marveling at the poverty and filth. Elves, he reminded himself, didn't build anything, and their lives were full of beauty and ease. So far, he hadn't seen any beauty in this life, and he suspected that ease didn't play much part in it, either.

Thorn and Willow dragged the heavy body to a nearby tree and tied it up by the front feet. Willow opened the crude door and spoke to someone inside. A minute later, an elf girl wandered out. She had lovely green eyes, the dirtiest hair Seylin had ever seen, and a miserable expression on her face.

"Not a deer!" she groaned. "And such a big one!"

The elf that Seylin had first met walked up behind her. "Don't you want to eat this winter, Irina?" he asked.

"It's all very well for you, Rowan," she grumbled. "He doesn't make you butcher them."

Elves normally slaughtered with a spell that took care of everything in typically beautiful fashion. The whole deer disappeared in a golden cloud and reappeared as neat parts. Irina took a large metal butcher knife and began to gut the deer into a tub. She was soon bloody to the elbows.

Thorn grinned. "You know the rule, puppy," he told her.

"Yeah," Willow chimed in, patting her cheek, "the ugly people have to butcher. That means you." She swatted his hand away from her face—since she was holding the knife, a dangerous move for them both. Seylin expected someone to laugh at Willow's joke, but no one did. He had, in fact, been stating their butchering rule, just the way Thorn had made it up.

"Well, come on," Thorn told the men, heading for the door of the hovel, but Seylin shook his head.

"I'll stay and help," he answered, pulling his elf knife from his belt. The men were puzzled at the offer. Irina was puzzled, too.

"Why is he helping, Thorn?" she demanded, peeling back the bloody deer hide. "He's not ugly. He looks better than any of you."

Thorn paused, staring thoughtfully at Irina, and then shot Seylin a suspicious glance. Why, indeed, should he stay out in the cold? The blond elf drew the obvious conclusion.

"It doesn't matter why," he growled, "because I think he's smart enough to keep that good-looking face of his out of trouble. It wouldn't look nearly so nice with two or three teeth missing."

Seylin's stomach was beginning to tie itself into knots. He couldn't believe he'd been searching for this. The pages may have teased him when he was a boy, but no one had ever made such a crude threat.

"I've been after that one," said Rowan thoughtfully, studying the carcass. "He was a smart old beast."

Seylin felt ashamed. "I'm not a very good hunter," he admitted. "I had to use a calling spell."

"I know," said Rowan. "I watched you. You're an awful hunter," he added matter-of-factly.

"I don't care what he is," remarked Thorn to the group. "He's brought home food, and that's more than some people around here have done lately. Seylin, stop stabbing at it. Butchering's not for men. You don't know what you're doing, and Irina has enough help."

Another woman had stepped up silently to join them, carving off strips of the haunch. Seylin didn't notice her arrival until she was kneeling almost at his feet. The busy woman had her back to him and didn't seem interested in introductions. Her long hair was black, so it didn't show dirt as badly as her companion's.

"Come on," said Thorn impatiently, and the men went into the warmth of the cave while the women worked in the cold.

Beyond the plank door was a big, messy room floored with dirt, half house and half cave. Along the back wall were four low tents, the only thing in the room that made sense. Elves always slept in tents, inside or outside.

There was a fireplace at the boarded front of the cave, with thick logs blazing in it. Seylin could look at the flames because his eyes weren't normal elf eyes, but he didn't understand how the other elves could bear it. Everything he had ever read about elves mentioned their hatred of fire and metal; they associated both things with goblins. Yet here, in a real elf camp, he saw a fire crackling merrily on a normal human hearth with a metal pot heating above it.

Seylin braced himself for the expected barrage of questions, but no one even bothered to speak to him. Thorn and Willow began scraping the bits of flesh off a deer hide, and Rowan sat down with a hunk of fat to grease his ancient boots. The perplexed newcomer occupied himself with pitching his own tent at the end of the row and settling his belongings into their places.

When he turned around, the women were back inside, preparing the morning meal. Irina was patting out dough with still-bloody hands and frying it up on a griddle. The black-haired woman had her back to him again, stirring the stewpot.

"Who is she?" he asked, joining the men. Thorn glanced up from his deer hide.

"That's the ugly woman," he replied. "Ugly woman! Show the nice man why we call you that."

The black-haired woman turned around, and Seylin had trouble avoiding a gasp. Her cheeks were covered by twisted masses of scar tissue. The smooth, perfect skin abruptly became silvery, pink, and white, in mottled, tangled bands across the sides of her face. The scar tissue tugged up one corner of her lip so that she always appeared to be smiling, but the dark blue eyes that she raised to his face were the saddest he had ever seen.

"It's unbelievable, isn't it?" commented the elf man, enjoying Seylin's shocked expression. "Ugly woman! Get that ghastly thing out of my sight."

Seylin watched her turn away again, her head bowed and her shoulders slumped. Goblin deformity was a deformity of strength, but this was unnatural and brutal. Why had this woman been disfigured? Why hadn't she been treated and healed? Seylin couldn't recall a single instance of the deliberate maiming of an elf.

"Food's ready," said Irina, and the men stood up. Thorn glanced down inquiringly at Seylin, but he was too upset to eat. He just shook his head.

Thorn walked forward to take the first bowl and a piece of bread from Irina. But when Rowan stepped forward to take the next bowl, Thorn blocked the way. He set down his own food and took the bowl himself, weighing it critically and putting part of it back into the pot. Then he took a piece of bread and laid it on the bowl.

"Puppy!" he said. "Here's your share."

"Oh," said the blond girl, surprised. "Thanks, Thorn," and she reached up to take the bowl. The scarred woman stared in astonishment at this and looked up at Rowan. He gave her a shrug in return, as if to say, Why would I care?

The scarred woman spooned Rowan's bowl and then scraped the pot to spoon Willow's, but Thorn took the bowl as Willow reached for it and faced the youngster sternly.

"When's the last time you've brought home food?" he wanted to know. "You need to go hungry for a few nights, Willow. When I was your age, I brought home my share."

"There's not much out there," muttered the youth. "It's not like I don't look."

"Rowan and I do all right," challenged the man. "We keep the lot of you fed." The boy just scowled in answer, staring at his boots.

"You still don't know what you're doing," commented Rowan from his seat on the floor, where he was rapidly devouring his stew. "Come with me on my next night, Willow. I'll help you find something."

Thorn handed over the stew, eyeing the young elf critically. "See that you bring something home next time," he ordered. Then he picked up his bowl and bread. He tore the bread in half and frowned at it.

"Ugly woman!" he said. "Come get your food."

The scarred woman stood up, her eyes on the strip of bread he held out. Her face was wary and her whole body tense. She reached out for the bread, but at the last second, he dropped it. Then he stepped on it as he walked back to his place.

Seylin glanced around in outrage, expecting someone to say something, but they were all busy with their food. What had happened was no business of theirs. He watched with distaste as the woman picked up her bread and quickly dusted it off. She knelt down next to the hearth again, eating it hurriedly, like an animal who has found a scrap that may be stolen at any second. He realized then that she had no bowl of stew. She began to scrape the remains out of the cooking pot, trying to make as little sound with the spoon as possible. Seylin watched her moodily. He could tell there wasn't much left.

"Doesn't she have a name?" he asked. Thorn followed his gaze to the woman at the hearth. When she realized they were talking about her, she dropped the spoon into the pot with a clatter and froze, her eyes on the ground.

"The ugly woman, you mean?" asked Thorn casually. "Oh, yes,

she has a name. A grand name, in fact, passed down from her father. Sable, his name was. We don't use that name now, out of respect for him. He wasn't the useless trash that she is. You'd never believe it, but that thing was engaged to me. I hunted for her when I was sixteen, Willow," he said, shaking a finger at the young elf. "You could take a lesson. I brought home two shares at sixteen, her share as well as my own. For years I took care of her, did everything for her, and then our marriage moon came. She'd never turned down a meal, notice. She hasn't turned down one since. But she told me on our wedding night that she wouldn't marry me. And then"—he pointed at the scarred cheeks—"that's what she did to her face."

Seylin gasped, wincing. "She did that to *herself*? Why?"

"Because she's a coward," snapped Thorn. "Because she wanted to stay a child. She took the most beautiful thing I've ever seen, and she destroyed it just to spite me. She killed my wife. I'm a widower, with a dead wife. But she eats more than most dead wives do. How I hate to see my good food disappear into that ugly face!"

Irina sat before Thorn on the floor, finishing her supper, her back turned to him, and her whole attention on the remaining food she had. His gray eyes bright with malice, Thorn reached out and tugged on a lock of her dirty hair.

"But puppy here's no coward, are you?" he said. "Six months from now is your marriage moon. That's when pretty elf girls find a husband, but I don't know about clumsy puppies. What do you think, puppy? Will there be a husband out there for you?"

Irina shrugged, not particularly interested. Husbands weren't something she knew much about, and she still had a little bread left. But Seylin saw Thorn watching his dead wife over Irina's shoulder, and he saw the scarred woman raise her blue eyes to stare at Thorn. The look that passed between them was pure, poisonous hatred. Thorn glared at her in malicious triumph, still tugging on the girl's hair.

"Ow, Thorn!" said Irina irritably. "You're hurting me!" She jerked away, completely unaware of the drama surrounding her.

"I'm going to sleep," muttered Seylin. "I'm tired." And he jumped up and headed for his tent before anyone could stop him with a question. But he needn't have worried. No one bothered to say anything. They didn't even look up.

He hid in his tent and listened to the elves preparing for sleep. No one bid the others good morning or pleasant dreams. Seylin lay there for a long time, thinking of home and what he had hoped to find. He hadn't found it here, and he was sure he never would. Grown men and members of the King's Guard weren't supposed to cry. He didn't, but he wished that he could.

Sable lay in her tent, next to the sleeping Irina, worrying about the new elf. Fine clothes, soft hands, well-made boots, and he claimed to be the last of his band. He didn't even eat with them. He'd never seen a single hungry night. Why didn't Thorn make him tell the truth? Her father would have dealt with that new elf. But, then, he'd have dealt with her, too.

Sable had never known her mother. For years, she hadn't even known that elves had mothers. Her father ran their camp. He was the handsomest man in it, and he had a hard pride because of the name that the two of them shared.

"Never forget, Sable," he would tell her firmly, "we aren't like these common idiots."

Sable was six when she saw and heard the first elf woman die. Rose moaned and screamed for two days in her tent. At the end of it, Sable and her friend Laurel held the tiny Irina, and the cold ground held Rose's bloody body. That was how babies were born, her father told her. The women had to die. Her mother lay under the ground, too, and so did countless other women. After that, Sable was sure she saw the dead women crawling through the camp looking for their babies. She woke up screaming from nightmare after night-mare, but when she told her father, he beat her. "Never tell those dreams to anyone," he ordered, and Sable never did.

Animals and birds raised their children together, but an elf woman had one happy year of marriage, and then she had to die. An elf man had to face the long years without her, raising their baby and finding food. But not all the men lived up to their part of the bargain. The night May died bearing Willow, her husband walked out of camp and never came back, and Rowan's father killed himself before his wife was even dead.

Sable's father kept on, strong and relentless. He drove himself unceasingly to make up for those cowardly fathers, to care for the children and teach them what they needed to know. He had buried two wives of his own, but he couldn't afford the luxury of dying. Not until Rowan and Thorn could hunt. Not until the camp could keep on. The long nights of work were hard, and they wore him down at last, but Father knew life wasn't for the weak.

Father had taught Sable about the goblins who trapped and enslaved elves, about the magical tortures they devised for their vic-tims. They had rounded up the elves who weren't brave enough to stand against them and had bred them into a race of monsters. That was a fitting end for a coward, Father had always said. Sable knew she was a coward.

Father had lived his difficult life and had met his responsibilities, but when her turn came, Sable had refused to die. She didn't want to lie cold and stiff while her baby cried. Sable wanted to live. She didn't mind what Thorn said about her, and she didn't mind what he fed her. She had made her choice, and she was grateful for her life. There were worse things than going hungry and eating dirty bread, and Sable knew what they were. Hideous tortures in caves under-ground. Gruesome spells. Goblins.

That night, Marak went to study Seylin's map on the wall of his workroom. It had been quite interesting of late: a fast, straight journey of several days, and then slow, deliberate sweeps back and forth in a small area. The goblin King frowned at the map, combing his fingers through his striped hair. At this point, Seylin was only about two nights' journey away. He was near human villages, but maybe there was enough cover to keep some elves happy. And he was on the border of the elf King's forest that was farthest away from the goblin kingdom. An elf band fleeing the harrowing might have stopped there and found life good.

Almost time, thought Marak. We'll see what he does tonight. If he's still there tomorrow, then I'll know what to do.

chapter Seven

Seylin woke up to screams, but before he could spring from his tent to help, the screams stifled themselves and fell silent. A loud voice began to curse nearby.

"Useless piece of trash!" it called. "Why didn't you cut your tongue out, too, and give us all a rest? Why didn't you cut your worth-less throat?" The scarred Sable had apparently had a nightmare, and her leader was responding as he thought best. Seylin climbed out of his tent, his spirits sinking. That's right, he remembered glumly. I've found elves.

"I spotted a burrow of hares near the three dead oaks," Rowan remarked to Thorn as they waited for the evening meal. "And I think I have an idea where a doe might be sheltering. What do you say to Willow's going out with me to kill the hares and help track the deer?"

"A doe," said Thorn, pleased. "That's a good plan. Willow, you go with Rowan, and if you find the doe, you won't have to hunt on your next night."

Seylin had walked over to the primitive hearth to watch Sable build the evening fire. The scarred woman had covered the embers with ashes to keep them alive throughout the day, but they had died down to almost nothing. Now she was carefully bringing the tiny coals back with dry needles, trying to rescue the fire without smoth-ering it. Seylin felt a little impatient at the slow process. It was cold in the damp, drafty cave.

"You're going to be here all night doing that," he observed, taking a large log and laying it behind the fragile embers. "Here." He reached out in the spell that normally heated the cooking stones. The log burst into a dramatic sheet of flame. Sable winced at the bright light and then began to pile on the rest of the logs. The room warmed up perceptibly.

"That's a handy spell to know," said Seylin as the other elves came over to look at his accomplishment. "Do you want to learn it?"

"No," grunted Thorn, turning away. "That's the ugly woman's job. I don't care if she spends all night puffing out her ugly cheeks to blow on a handful of twigs." Rowan had looked interested, but he declined to speak after that.

"What about you, Sable?" persisted Seylin. "Wouldn't you like to learn it?" The other elves burst out laughing.

"That's a good one!" chortled Rowan, walking away. "Wouldn't she love it! Sure, teach her!"

"And while you're at it," said Thorn with a laugh, "teach her how to track and hunt, and not look like a fright."

"Yeah, ugly woman," jeered Willow. "Show us your magic. Show us all the spells you can do."

Sable continued to build her fire, her back to the other elves. She didn't even look as if she'd heard. But she glanced up at Seylin for the barest of instants, and he saw the hurt reproach in her eyes. He walked away, depressed and confused. Why couldn't she learn spells? Was it some strange flaw in her character, the same one that had led her to the mutilation? Maybe she was truly insane and was normal or mad by turns. Elves didn't suffer delusions, but their sensitive natures could give way under strain.

Once again, Thorn gave Irina her food.

"It's all right," she told him, nonplussed. "I can get it for myself."

"No, you can't," he said, walking back to sit down with his own bowl. It began to dawn on Irina that something must be going on.

"Why do you keep giving me my food?" she demanded.

"Go ask your father," answered the blond elf, busy eating.

Irina considered this carefully.

"How can I do that?" she wanted to know. "Father isn't buried at this camp."

Rowan and Thorn laughed at this, but Sable didn't laugh. Neither did Willow, who, intent on his food, hadn't been listening. And neither did Seylin. He was having a hard time making it through his food. The dried deer meat was tough and slightly moldy, and the unevenly cooked round of bread had no salt in it at all. This was something that Lore-Master Webfoot had stressed. The elf diet was very monotonous. The food changed seasonally, depending on which fruits and vegetables were available, but the basic structure of the meals hadn't changed for thousands of years. Seylin bit into the lumpy bread and tried not to grimace. This was just one more aspect of elf culture he had failed to take into account.

He became aware that the scarred woman wasn't eating like the rest. She was quietly stitching something made of rabbit skins.

"Isn't Sable going to eat?" he demanded.

"No," said Thorn, tearing apart a piece of meat with his fingers. "If she wants food, she can keep her mouth shut the next time we're trying to get some sleep."

Sable kept stitching as if she hadn't heard, trying to ignore her hunger. Her mind kept drifting to the deer meat in the little shed outside. The last time Thorn had caught her stealing from the winter stores, he had made her eat frozen, raw meat for days. It hadn't tasted bad, but it had made her terribly cold.

The night was clear and frosty. Rowan and Willow wrapped their patched cloaks around themselves and headed out into the icy forest. Sable, Thorn, and Irina settled down to work, and Seylin felt left out. He wondered how this band had survived the harrowing and had then gone on to lose its language. They seemed to know something about magic, but he hadn't seen them work a single spell.

"Do you know anything about your band's history?" he asked the three busy elves. Thorn glanced up from his deer hide.

"You mean when elves were born and died, that kind of thing? The ugly woman's got a book about it. If you want, she can show it to you."

Sable rose and went back to her tent to get the book.

"We can look at it here," she said very quietly, crouching down with it by the tents. Her voice was clear and sweet, an odd contrast to her ghastly face. Seylin noticed that she was as far from Thorn as she could be. They were also as far from the firelight as they could be, and Seylin's unelvish eyes had trouble making out the writing on the cover. He snapped his fingers absently, and a little gibbous moon appeared over his shoulder, shedding its faint light. Sable stared at it in wonder for a few distracted seconds while Seylin examined the front of the book. *Top Shield Star Camp, Volume 42,* read the cover.

"Sable!" he exclaimed in excitement. "It's a camp chronicle!"

"Yes," agreed the elf woman, misunderstanding him, "it tells all about what happened in our camp. It was my father's book, and he wrote in it whenever someone was born or died. My father knew how to write," she added with wistful pride. "I wanted to learn, but he taught Thorn instead. He said it wasn't for women."

She glanced at Seylin for confirmation of this, but Seylin just looked confused. It was true that the nomadic elf society, based on the male hunter, was more rigid in its gender differences than goblin society was, but he knew that elf girls normally learned to write because certain kinds of chronicling and magic belonged exclusively to the women.

"Anyway," she continued in a low voice, "Thorn hasn't kept it up. He should have written in it when Laurel died, but he said he didn't need to waste the time. We all knew she was dead, he said, so why write it down?"

Sable held the camp chronicle in her lap. The book was her only treasure. Even Thorn wouldn't have damaged her father's book, although she took care not to let him see how much she loved it. She ran her fingers affectionately over the old cover. She even liked the smell of it.

"Nine different people have written in the book," she told Seylin. "I know by the way they write. See, this one's so beautiful," she said, running her finger over the writing on the first page. The eager Seylin wished she would get her hand out of the way. "... in the six-teenth year of the reign of Aganir U-Sakar ..." caught his eye. The elf King named New Moon. That was the last elf King. This chronicle began over two hundred years ago.

"And look," she said, turning the page before he could make out anything else, "here's my name." She put her finger on it. Seylin looked at the page.

... waxed strong and bold now that our King is dead, and they came on this the third night from the second full moon of spring. But because their evil King was not with them, I led my warriors against them and rescued fourteen of the maid-ens they had taken. And when dawn came, we gathered the living and found that we had, besides the forty-two married women and widows, still twenty-seven warriors, twenty-two boys not yet of age, the fourteen maidens, and eight girl chil-dren, down to the youngest baby. And, perceiving that we could not sustain another attack, but that we would next time fail, I, Lord Sabul, have led my people away this night. But yet is our flight desperate, for we have not the proper stores, nor books of spells, nor dare we risk contacting the other camps, which may no longer be, for all we know. ...

"See?" said the scarred woman, looking up. "That's my name, Sable. Father showed me once. Doesn't it look pretty? I know how to write it, I've practiced with a stick in the ashes."

Seylin tore himself away from the grim tale of the elf harrowing to look at her. She was the direct descendant of Lord Sabul, noble leader of one of the elf King's eighteen camps, and she couldn't even read her own family history.

"Your name is pretty," he confirmed solemnly. "Did you know your ancestors ruled a camp?" He meant that they were lords under the elf King, but again Sable misunderstood.

"Oh, yes," she assured him. "A Sable has always run this camp until now. My father ran it until he died when I was twelve. He always told me that we weren't like the rest of these"—she hesitated— "common idiots."

Seylin thought of the last Lord Sabul ruling a camp of five or six elves. He looked at Sable's filthy, bloodstained clothes, her mutilated face, the wary look in her eyes. What an end to this proud line.

"And over here," she added, turning the pages before he could read anything at all, "here's my name again, in the middle of a story. Something bad happened, I know, maybe a battle because after that the handwriting's never so nice again."

"Let me see, Sable," he said. "I'll tell you what happened." He studied the page.

. . . and because the men were hauling flour and the children were gathering nuts with the young maidens, the women were alone in the caves with only two guards. Having lost all but one cooking stone, and being cold, the women made a fire with logs for warmth, but although it did not burn their bodies, yet this evil force, this goblin thing, reached out in some hideous way to strangle the breath out of them. And when we returned for the morning meal, here were my wife and thirty other women besides, dead within the inner caves. And the worst is not yet told, and I, Lord Sabul, am to blame, for with these women has died also the women's craft and art, for those who survived because they were out gathering, these did not know what the other women knew, and I had never seen to it that these things be written down. And I stood at the grave with my elves and watched the little girls crying for their mothers, and better would it be for these children if I slit their throats this night. But now we must seek human women to enslave for the sake of these children and the children who will come after. No worse calamity has visited us in the last one hundred years, and this night has died my camp with the women, though that dying will take long.

Seylin paused in his reading. What had died with the women? Spells, perhaps. Certainly they would have lost the making of elf clothes then. He wished he could show the book to Marak. The goblin King would know.

"It wasn't a battle, Sable," he said, "but you're right that it was bad." He stopped at the look on her face.

"You know how to read," she whispered. Her father knew how to write, but she had never seen him look at his own book this way, as if he were talking with the writers who were dead. This strange young elf who knew so much magic was the master of her book. He looked offended and perplexed at her comment and the serious, frightened look that went with it.

"Well, yes, I know how to read. It's not so hard, really, or at least it wouldn't be if you knew how to speak elvish. This is all written in elvish, you know." She continued to study him fearfully, so he sighed and turned the page.

The handwriting changed abruptly. The letters were poorly formed, the entries short. He frowned for a long minute over a passage before he could understand it. The writer was mixing elvish and English in the most bizarre fashion. All he could gather was that several slaves had escaped because the Camp Spell broke. That must have been the last time they had a properly working camp perimeter.

On the next page, he found little more than lists of births and deaths. New handwriting, and the elvish numbers and dates were gone. Now the entries were nothing but English written very clumsily in the elvish phonetic hooking script. Some of them were almost impossible to decipher. He read one out loud, running his finger under the line, and Sable came to his rescue.

"That's from my grandfather," she said. "My father told me about it, when the last slave died. She was an old human woman who raised the children. All the other slaves were long gone because by then they could get away, but she stayed because she'd been there since she was young and she loved the children so. My father said the whole band, more than twenty of them there were then, they cried for days when she died. She was like the mother to the whole camp, that woman, and Father said he never cried so hard for an elf as he did when that ugly old human died.

"Here's my father's writing," she continued, turning the page, and Seylin stared in dismay. Only the most rudimentary of elf characters sounded out the English names. Instead of "born," a star next to the name. Instead of "dead," a cross. A human must have taught her father that—maybe the old human woman he remembered so fondly. Here were the elves of the current camp. Rowe, Rowan. Laharil, Laurel, that was the woman whose death Thorn had failed to record. And then, somewhat crude, but confident and clear, the name of Lord Sabul, with a star for birth and a stick figure in a dress to show the gender.

"That's me," said Sable, touching it with her finger. "That's when I was born."

Seylin shifted on the cave floor and flipped back to the first page, with its elegant, curling script and capable, crisp prose. And then to the last. Scrawled English names, symbols, and picture writing. Blots and scratches on the page. He imagined the last Lord Sabul sitting in this filthy cave in his filthy rags, trying his best to carry on the lord's duty of updating the camp chronicles. And now they didn't even have a lord. The camp leader was nothing more than its meanest, toughest member, ruling because of his ambition and his fists. Seylin shook his head sadly as he flipped through the pages again. Nine generations since the death of the last elf King, and the Top Shield Star Camp was finished.

He glanced up out of his reverie to meet a pair of stern blue eyes and was surprised at the look of authority he saw. Perhaps he'd started lamenting the end of the elves too soon. The daughter of the last Lord of the Top Shield Star Camp wasn't finished yet.

"You know how to read, how to work spells we don't know, and how to speak elvish," she said quietly. "Your clothing is well made, and you almost have more of it than we have in the whole rest of our camp."

"Yes," confirmed Seylin.

"But you say you're the last elf," she added, carefully watching his face.

"Yes," insisted Seylin unhappily. He was in for it now.

"Thorn is wrong about you," she said. "Your women aren't dead. Such fine clothing—there were many women weaving and sewing where you came from."

"Where I came from, the men worked weaving and sewing as well as the women," said Seylin. "Thorn's not wrong. I'm alone. I lost the woman I loved."

"Who did you lose her to?" asked Sable. The young elf wouldn't answer. She watched him for a moment, but he didn't meet her eyes.

"You're a danger," she concluded. "Or you bring danger. I can feel it. My father would have driven you out of camp."

"Then your father would have made a mistake," declared Seylin. "I only want to help. I can teach you things. Elvish and spells, things to help you survive."

The scarred woman shook her head.

"Thorn won't let you teach anything. If he doesn't know it, he won't learn it from you, and he won't let us learn it. He's the best hunter and the best fighter, and that's how he wants it. You should leave, Seylin. There's no place for you here."

She got up quickly, put the book away, and went back to her work. Seylin sat where she had left him, in the shadow of the tents. There was no place for him here. There was no place for him anywhere. The only place he belonged was with Emily, and he had lost that place forever. I should have sat on her couch and argued with her all day long, he thought. I should have changed into a cat and then danced for her. How could I have let her go so easily, over a little pride? How could I have run away and let her marry Thaydar?

Em, what are you doing now? he wondered. Do you ever think about me? I want to come home to you.

⸺

Emily was having problems of her own. She hadn't been to London since she was a little girl. She had plenty of money and plenty of things to see, and she had expected to enjoy herself thoroughly, but her dour goblin companion was ruining all her fun. Everywhere they went, Ruby quoted appropriate facts from her lessons, but she didn't seem impressed by anything. All she saw was filth and ineptitude. Emily was running out of patience.

They were walking along in the twilight by the handsome old

buildings of Parliament. The smoke of thousands of dinner fires hung in the still sky, and crowds of people tugged them to and fro. Changed into her normal shape and carefully hooded, Ruby stomped along the brick pavement.

"Humans," she remarked with grim satisfaction. "Mercy! How they do smell!"

"Didn't you think that Westminster Abbey was beautiful?" asked the young woman, trying not to notice a withered beggar who kept thrusting a hand in her face.

"The burial place of Chaucer," grunted Ruby. "And most of the English kings." Emily waited, but Ruby said nothing more. She took that to mean no.

"What about Saint Paul's Cathedral?" she inquired. "You can't tell me that wasn't astounding!"

"Designed in the baroque style by Christopher Wren," intoned the teacher, "who died in 1723. The dome is higher than the goblin King's throne room. Of course, Wren wasn't trying to fit it underground. It pleased the eye, I suppose, but it's nothing like what the dwarves could have made."

"Ruby, that's just it!" exclaimed Emily in annoyance. "The dwarves didn't build it, and magic didn't, either. We humans made it with our own hands and tools, out of our own minds. We made it the hard way. Doesn't that mean anything to you?"

"I'd say that one fine building out of all this mess is hardly worth tears of joy," snapped the old goblin. "You humans run around all day long creating chaos and trouble, and then you want credit for every little good work."

"But you don't know what it's like to be a human," insisted Emily, shouldering her way past a chestnut vendor's stand. "We aren't like you goblins. We don't have a magical king to make sure we do the right things. You do whatever you're told, but we have to decide what we should do. It's a hard life, and no one looks after us. If we do any good at all, that's saying something."

The goblin woman stopped walking, struck by this line of reasoning.

"I hadn't thought about that," she said slowly. "You don't have anyone to help you. I don't think I'd want to be a human. It sounds terribly lonely."

"There, you see—" began Emily in triumph, but she didn't have time to finish. Ruby gave a cry of fury and caught a passing boy by the hand.

"This is exactly what I expect from humans!" she exulted with delighted wrath. "Just as soon as I begin to see good in them, a smelly little thief pops up. Come here, young man," she ordered, dragging the culprit to the edge of the crowd. "I'll teach you to pick my pocket! I'm going to give you a lesson you'll never forget!" And, standing close to a lighted window, she threw back her hood.

Her victim gave a squawk of surprise. Then he burst out laughing. He reached up his free hand and plucked the big battered hat from his head.

The boy might have been around ten, but it was hard to be sure. His grimy face and ragged frame were terribly thin, and he was twisted over by a badly hunched back. His greasy hair looked as if it might turn out to be white, and his eyes were a penetrating golden-green. His sharp ears flipped over at the tips, and his widely grinning mouth showed one fang, the matching fang having fallen victim to a fistfight. The hand holding the hat didn't end in fingertips. It ended in inch-long claws.

"You're ugly as me, ma'am!" he crowed joyfully. "You're ugly enough to be my mum!"

Ruby stared in amazement at her elated captive, almost unable to move.

"I don't know what this means," she muttered in shock.

"I do," volunteered Emily, examining their find. "Your smelly little human thief is a goblin."

The two bemused women took their prisoner to the nearest public house and watched him wolf down a plateful of sausages. Emily had never seen food disappear so fast without the aid of magic.

"What's your name?" demanded Ruby in her sternest classroom voice. "Where are your parents? Who's your mother?"

The child studied his empty plate philosophically and pushed it away with a sigh. "The name's Richard," he answered. "I've got no parents. Never did have, as a matter of fact."

Emily nudged her companion. "His father must be one of the goblin men from the trading journeys."

"Impossible!" declared her former teacher. "Goblins don't behave like that! At least, they almost never—well, I didn't think they did—oh, I don't know what to think."

"Don't mind me," recommended the urchin in mollifying tones. "No need to get upset. Thank you kindly for the fodder. I'd better be getting back."

He stood up to go, but Ruby came to herself with a jerk. "You sit down," she ordered firmly. "I have to decide what to do. I'll need to send a message to the King at once. Oh, dear! I've almost forgotten how to do that."

"The king!" Richard's pale green eyes widened in distress. "There's no call to involve the authorities, is there, now? I've not harmed you, you've not harmed me, it was all just a bit of convivial good sport."

Emily smiled at the youngster's appealing tone. "We're not talking about the same king you know. We—or rather, you and Ruby— you have a different king."

Richard digested this information. A whole new world opened up before him.

"You mean ugly people have a king all their own?" he whispered.

"Yes, we do," confirmed Ruby. "He doesn't know about you yet, but he'll want to see you right away."

The skinny boy couldn't contain his astonishment. "You don't mean meet me?" he marveled. "Me? A king and all? Standing in the same room? 'Hello, Richard, how's the lad,' and a friendly slap on the back?"

"I hardly think he'll slap it," said the teacher with a frown. "He'll want to start mending it right away. I've never seen such a bad back before. It's going to take months before you can stand up straight."

Richard gawked at her for a few seconds, but he was a wise boy. He didn't waste time on questions.

"All right," he announced in a businesslike tone. "If a king's that anxious to see me, I won't be the one to say nay. But I have to go get my family. I'm not leaving them behind." He stood up and made for the door.

"Family!" exclaimed Ruby.

"You said you didn't have parents," protested Emily, catching up to him.

"No more have I, but a man's got to have a family." He led the way through the crowd outside.

They followed Richard up narrow streets and down little alleys and through the closed lanes that led from one tangle of decrepit buildings to another. He dragged them through a tiny opening, up some steps, through an attic that connected several apartments, down a ladder, along a cellar wall, and then up more dangerous stairs into another little attic.

There, in the dusky twilight glow coming through a tiny, paper-covered window, the two women found the goblin child's family. A little human boy and girl lay asleep on a filthy blanket, twins no more than six years old. Ruby knelt down and lit a goblin flame to study them. It accented their strawberry-blond hair and played up the rosy color of their thin cheeks.

"I found Jack and Martha crying in a cellar," Richard explained. "I've taken care of them since they could barely talk. I'm teaching Jack the trade because a man's got to have a profession, but I don't let 'em run any risks. Say, Jack," he said, nudging the boy, and the children awoke, blinking at the newcomers gravely.

"What's up, Rich?" asked the little boy. "Who's the green lady?"

"Guess what I've found!" said Richard in excitement. "A bunch of people just like me!"

"Pretty hair," said little Martha with a happy smile. She stood up and stretched out one small hand to pat the astonished Ruby on her bun.

"That's my family," announced Richard to his new companions. "Aren't they beautiful?" he added wistfully.

"They certainly are," said Emily. "They're as nice a family as anyone could want."

Ruby put her arms around the young twins, and the sleepy children cuddled up to her, sharing the warmth of her cloak. She held them close in breathless wonder. Ruby had finally found something in the human world to love.

chapter Eight

Sleet fell outside the elves' cave, and an icy wind blew through the
bare trees. Although it was twilight, the forest was already very dark.
Thorn was angry at Sable because she had had another nightmare
and had woken them up with her screams. At the evening meal, he
once again made sure that she had no food.

The meal finished, each found some indoor activity to do. Willow continued scraping hides, Thorn began cutting out leather
pieces for a new pair of boots, and Rowan sat cross-legged, sewing
another patch onto his heavily patched tunic. Sable continued
stitching rabbit skins together, probably to make the lining of a new
winter cloak. She wouldn't be the one to wear it, Seylin thought
gloomily. Her own clothes were so old and tattered that they would
have been little use as rags.

Irina knelt by the cave wall, weaving the shuttle of a hand loom
back and forth. The loom was nothing more than two long rods
with holes bored in them. Coarse yarn had been threaded through
these holes like the many strings of a harp. Irina pushed the shuttle
across the row, over one string, under the next, pulling yarn between
them. At the end of each line, she tamped her yarn down against all
the other lines below it, and the cloth was bigger by the thickness of
that piece of yarn. Watching her drudge her way through the slow
work, Seylin realized why the elves' clothing was so frightful.

Seylin himself had no work to do. His clothes didn't need patch-
ing, and he didn't need to repair anything. He didn't really want to

learn how to scrape a hide, either, so he decided to oil his boots. He buffed off the dirt with a towel, took a small flask from his pack, and began to rub oil into the leather. When it came right down to it, he thought, he was just playing at being a member of this band, pretending to take part in a life-style that meant survival or death to them. There's no place for you here, Sable had said. He knew that she was right.

"Seylin?" He jumped guiltily, but it was only Irina speaking from her loom. "Did your band know any new stories?" She turned around to look at him, her smudged face eager and her green eyes bright. "Do you know something different? We just know the same old boring stories we've always told."

"He hasn't heard our stories," observed Rowan. "How's he supposed to know if his stories are new or old and boring?"

"Don't be mean," pouted Irina, missing the point entirely. "Come on, Seylin, tell us something new."

"And make sure we haven't heard it before," prompted Rowan, grinning at Thorn.

Now, this was something that Seylin could provide. He recalled his favorite tales. What might they not know?

"Do you know the story of the last elf King's Wife?" he asked. Irina shook her head. That was a nice story, then, and gracefully told in the elvish chronicles.

"This took place in the reign of Marak Whiteye and Aganir U-Sakar, the elf King named New Moon. New Moon, the last elf King, was handsome and vain, a moody and fickle King. Born not from love, but from the hatred of his father and mother, he had no interest in the trials of marriage and long remained alone. Condemned, as all the Kings before him, to marry a human bride, he rebelled against the thought of bringing home someone with such imperfect looks, and his advisers proposed different women to him without success. So went the battle, year after year, until the eigh-teenth year of his reign, when the master of Hallow Hill brought home his own bride to wed in the chapel on his estate.

"The young master, William, and Belinda, his betrothed, were deeply in love with each other. They had not yet exchanged marriage vows, but they had already sealed their promise of love with a pair of golden lockets. While their friends danced, William and Belinda wandered together under the moon, lost to everything else. As they talked about the lifetime of happiness they would share, the elf King watched them from the shadows of the forest. He studied that lovely young face, alight with joy, and his proud heart was satisfied. After years of stubborn waiting, he had found what he wanted. Here was a human woman whose looks would not disgrace him.

"The elves stole Belinda on the night before her wedding, and her new bridegroom was displeased at the bitter tears she shed. As the women led her away to prepare her for the ceremony, she begged to keep her locket, but the King just laughed and assured her that she wouldn't want it long. After the ceremony, he gave her the drink that would take away her former life. She cried as she drank it but stopped when she put the goblet down. New Moon's face was the first thing she saw, and she remembered nothing else. The elf King took her hand and danced with her among his court, and Belinda shed no more tears for her lost William.

"But Aganir U-Sakar and his bride were not happy for long. The amnesia drink of the later elf Kings' Wives is blamed for the destruction of the kingdom, and it played its evil part in this romance. It found favor with the proud, sensitive Kings because it forced their human brides to love them. Yet this adoration came with a childish dependence since their empty lives held nothing else, and the elf Kings found that their vacuous wives had nothing interesting to say. Every King who used the amnesia drink on his bride soon abandoned her, and the pain this caused the poor human women, who had lost every other possession, was a sad and touching spectacle to see. The other elves tended to avoid the intruders as well, and so these humans led a tragic life, with no place at all in the only world they knew, and no memory of the world where they belonged.

"But Belinda surprised her husband in two ways. First, and most important, she bore him no son. The whole reason for the bothersome marriage failed to put in an appearance. And, second, Belinda didn't adore her royal spouse. She didn't belong to him body and soul. Belinda had found a little golden locket shining in the grass. She thought it very beautiful but tremendously puzzling, for it held her own name and the picture of a man she had never seen. The elf King's Wife hid this precious find, and she looked and looked for the man who matched the picture. He remained a mystery, but he loomed very large in her life.

"The elf King soon realized that his wife didn't love him. In fact, he never tried to win her love. But he contrasted her expression as she looked at him with the look of love she had given her William, and the proud King began to grow resentful. Devastated by his loss, the master of Hallow Hill walked the grounds of his estate, a silent and stricken figure. The elf King came sometimes to watch the unhappy man, and he burned with angry jealousy. He had everything poor William had ever wanted, but the human man still held Belinda's heart.

"One night, the elf King's Wife was roaming the forest, singing to herself, and her human sweetheart heard that dear voice and followed it to his lost bride. Belinda never saw her lover because the elf guards saw him first, and they brought him back to camp as their prisoner. Face to face with his adversary, the elf King gave way to his injured pride and resolved upon a magical revenge. He changed the master of Hallow Hill into an antlered stag and hunted the beast himself.

"Close to dawn, the elf King returned to camp, bearing his fresh kill. 'See how well I've hunted for you,' he called to his wife. Belinda came obediently, delighted at the attention because her husband didn't often speak to her. While the King talked with his elves, she examined the dead stag politely. It soon held her complete attention. High on its neck, under the hair, she saw a locket shining. Within the locket was a man's name, William, and beside it was a picture of her.

"What happened next will always remain a mystery. Perhaps the Amnesia Spell broke, and Belinda remembered her old life, or perhaps she just guessed enough of it to find the truth. And no one knows how she did what she did because she was protected by powerful magic. But Belinda dusted off her hands and walked to the elf King's side. As her husband watched, well pleased with his night's work, she pulled his knife from his belt. She stabbed it between her ribs and into her heart, and she was dead before he could even stop smiling.

"The elf King raged at the shallow ingratitude of this woman whom he had favored with a royal marriage, and he refused when his advisers begged him to choose another. Within the year, he met with misfortune and died childless, and the race of elves died with their last King."

Seylin glanced up as he spoke the final words of the story and came back to the present with a jolt. In this room were five examples of the death of that race: rude, half-starving, helpless, disfigured, hateful, ignorant elves. Seylin looked at their puzzled faces, their filthy, pathetic clothes, the unremitting, harsh labor that kept their rough hands busy. They wouldn't even be able to speak to the old elves: they didn't know their own language.

"I don't believe that story," blurted out Rowan with a thoughtful frown. "The elf King would be a half-breed if his mother was a human, and I can't believe the elves would have a half-breed King."

"It isn't like that," said Seylin, "because the King's magic makes his marriage different from the others, and without—"

"I don't understand what the fuss was," interrupted Irina carelessly. "Wasn't the elf King handsome? Any elf would look better than her stupid human. I think she was just mean. She should be happy he brought her a deer."

"Maybe she had to butcher it," suggested Thorn, winking at Rowan.

"Maybe she couldn't stand the thought of butchering one more deer," prompted Rowan with a grin.

"Oh," said Irina. "I guess that makes sense, then. But don't you know anything like the good old stories, Seylin? You know, like the one where the goblin King kills the elf King?"

"What?" cried Seylin. "That's not possible! The goblin King can't kill the elf King—at least, not in a fair fight."

"Sure, he does," she said. "I can't believe you don't know that one. See, the goblin King was sneaking around the camp at night disguised as a huge black cat with eyes of fire, sucking the life out of the little elf girls. And the elf King caught him. And there was a big battle, and the goblin King killed him, and then, while they all watched in stunned amusement, he disappeared in a ball of flame."

"Stunned *amazement*," said Willow. "Irina, you're so stupid!"

"Oh, shut up, brat," she replied calmly. "It's all the same thing."

Seylin could have pointed out that not even a goblin King could sneak into a properly protected elf camp because the Camp Spell allowed only elves to enter freely. He could also have mentioned that the last thing a goblin King would wish was the deaths of little elf girls, who would otherwise grow up to be useful goblin brides. But, instead, he fixed on one small detail of the story.

"A huge black cat?" he demanded, rather startled.

"With eyes of fire," Irina assured him happily. "Doesn't it sound just horrible?"

"A goblin couldn't have eyes of fire," argued Willow. "If he did, he couldn't see."

"Seylin?" It was Sable's voice. "Tell us about the goblins."

Seylin looked at her, completely thunderstruck. How could she possibly have guessed?

"Now, why do you want to know about goblins, you witch?" jeered Thorn. "Goblins are just a tale to frighten children."

"No, he's seen them. Haven't you?" she demanded.

Seylin glanced around in dismay. The other elves were studying him with curiosity. Had he really seen goblins? What did they look like? Irina already had her mouth open to ask. But, fortunately for him, and unfortunately for Sable, Thorn lost his temper.

"Shut up, or I'll shut you up!" he roared. "I don't care if he has seen goblins! I don't care if he's a goblin himself! He brings home food, and that's a far sight more than you've ever done. You just sit around and eat it and give the rest of us indigestion. Goblins would just love your nasty face. I hope they come and take you off my hands, you ugly hag."

Sable cowered down over her sewing. Taken by goblins! There was no worse threat. Never to see the moon and stars again, never to be free. Endless torment, horrible experiments, and dying to bring a monster into the world. Surely not goblins! Nothing so horrible as that.

The elves were silent and morose after their leader's outburst. They didn't speak for the remainder of the night. Thorn stayed angry and irritable. At the morning meal he gave Sable the smallest strip of bread to eat, and he glared at her so fiercely that she didn't risk scraping the stewpot. As soon as the meal was over and chores were done, he walked to the door of the cave and gestured to her.

"Go sleep somewhere else," he ordered, pointing at the door. Sable glanced back toward her tent and hesitated. "Now!" snapped the elf leader. She walked to the door. She had no tent, no cloak, and no blanket.

Seylin jumped up in a fury. "Where is she supposed to go?" he demanded.

"Wherever she won't wake me up screaming like some insane owl," said Thorn. "She can't go far enough."

"But she's not safe out there!" insisted Seylin heatedly.

"Well, she's not safe in here," retorted Thorn. "Screaming day after day! I'm going to throttle her if she wakes me up again."

Sable looked from one to the other of the two angry men. She couldn't imagine any good outcome for her, regardless of the conclusion of the argument. She went through the door, and Seylin's heart sank. How could he do anything for her if she didn't want his help?

"Wait," he called. He took off his cloak and gave it to her. Then he stood and watched the black-haired woman walk purposefully into the dawn. She must have some shelter in mind. This must happen fairly often. Thrown out into the daylight! And she wouldn't even have had a cloak for warmth or shade from the sun if he hadn't been there. Seylin heaved a sigh and turned away. He wasn't sure how much longer he could stand this place.

Marak stood in the workroom in front of the maps, his unmatched eyes shrewd and thoughtful. He'd checked three times last night, and Seylin was still in exactly the same spot. Either he needed some sort of help, or he had found what he was looking for. Marak's eyes gleamed at the thought. Elves. Elf brides. If only he had! Finding new elf brides in this day and age would be the most important event of his whole reign.

The goblin King took the ring he had made out of Seylin's hair and walked to the big cave that held his water mirror. Then he tossed the ring against the liquid wall. It floated on the water, raising no ripples on its dark surface.

Marak sat down on the hard floor of the cave and leaned against the stone wall, reaching up to the floating object. He put the index finger of his right hand through the ring, the other fingers curling around it. His fingers felt cold in the frigid water. Only the index finger did not. It felt instead the soft locks of Seylin's hair as he lay asleep in his tent in the elves' cave. Marak concentrated on the sleeping form that was so far away. Then he closed his own eyes in sleep— or at least in something very like it.

Seylin dreamed that morning that he was back home again. He was sitting with Marak in the library, and he was telling the goblin King all about his travels. He described the five elves and their horrible life, their appalling ignorance, their pitiful clothes, and their struggle to find food.

It felt so good to be back home, talking over his troubles with a real friend. Marak listened carefully and asked him endless questions. Particularly about the women. Most particularly about Sable.

"She doesn't know any magic at all, you say," the King mused. "But it sounds like none of them knows very much. A camp lord's daughter! One of the high families. Tell me, does she have dark eyes?"

"No," said Seylin. "They're blue like Kate's, but her hair is black."

"Oh," said Marak, disappointed. "Maybe I'm wrong. Maybe the line has lost its strength. Black hair, though. I wonder what her parents looked like. No father; no mother, either. For any of them, come to think of it. Doesn't that strike you as strange?"

"The life must be too hard," said Seylin. "They must not live very long."

"Maybe so. And she's never been married, you're sure about that. Why not? What did they say about it?"

Seylin frowned. "Thorn said she was a coward. He said she wanted to stay a child."

"It takes courage to marry?" asked the goblin King. "What is that supposed to mean? What sort of life does a child have that would be worth keeping? That other girl's still a child by their standards, and she works as hard as any of them."

"I think it must be some sort of insanity," said Seylin, "to cause an injury like that to her face. I've never seen such massive wounds in my life. I'm surprised she survived it."

Marak combed his hand through his shock of striped hair, remembering his first wife.

"There are all kinds of insanity, I suppose," he reflected, "but the insanity I know doesn't match this case. Sable's patient under abuse, and she's using a good brain to observe and draw accurate conclusions. That goblin comment is remarkable! You're not fooling her at all. Truly insane people are not pleasant to be around, and they're a lot of work to care for. No, Sable's useful to them, that's why they keep her alive."

"Poor Sable," sighed the young man, shaking his head. The goblin King glanced up in sudden interest.

"Poor Sable?" he echoed. "Have you taken a fancy to that one?"

Seylin grimaced at the bluntness of the question. "She's really ugly," he protested.

The King studied him thoughtfully. This from someone who had grown up with goblins. "She probably doesn't have to be," he suggested calmly, but Seylin didn't look enthusiastic. "All right, what about the other one?"

"Irina?" asked Seylin. He grimaced again.

Marak continued to study his young subject. Perhaps all elves were this squeamish, he considered. No wonder their marriages were arranged years in advance.

"Never mind," he said. "Things are bound to improve. You're just getting to know them, after all. Maybe they'll grow on you."

The young man lapsed into silence. The goblin King watched him. "Was there something else, Seylin?" he prompted. "Anything else you wanted to tell me?"

"Not really," Seylin replied. "Only, just—I just wondered . . . Marak, how is Em?"

The goblin King grinned affectionately at that miserable face. Then he broke into an amused chuckle.

When Kate walked into the water-mirror cave a minute later and shook her sleeping husband, he still had a pleased smile on his face. He opened his strange eyes and focused on her slowly, squinting up from his hard resting place. He pulled his six-fingered hand from the surface of the mirror. Water dripped from five fingers, but the sixth was completely dry. He continued to smile absently as he flexed the fingers. They were so cold. He was so stiff. He'd been there for a long time.

"Marak," said the astonished Kate, kneeling beside him, "what on earth are you doing on the floor?"

Elves, thought the goblin King in satisfaction, looking at her. Pretty things, elves. Particularly this elf. Life is good, he thought.

"Kate," he said agreeably, "some spells are harder than others." He winced as he shifted on the stone floor. She watched him in concern.

"It's time for my magic lesson," she reminded him, "but do you want to wait until later?"

"Yes, I do," he said, climbing slowly to his feet and leaning on her as he limped to his workroom. "I don't have time for lessons right now."

He pulled Seylin's ring from his finger and studied it fondly. Then he took Emily's ring from its hook and laid them together in the palm of his hand. He cupped his other hand over them and whispered softly for a minute.

"I need to meet with Thaydar immediately on a military matter," he explained to his wife, hanging the two rings back up on one hook. "Besides, I can't risk you trying to kill me today, you mad elf. As tired as I am, you might succeed."

Meanwhile, Sable curled up beneath the sheltering bows of a yew tree and pulled Seylin's cloak over her face. She lay awake, think-ing about that new elf and Thorn's wish, and winced and shifted on the bare ground. Taken by goblins. A goblin's bride. Please, nothing so horrible as that!

Life is good, she thought fervently, rubbing her cold hands to warm them. Please don't let the goblins come. Please let me stay up here where there are stars.

Chapter Nine

Another boring night was almost over. Seylin studied his map to pass the time. He wanted to read the camp chronicle, but he didn't want Sable to start talking about goblins again. He needed to find a time to ask her about that when no one else was nearby.

Rowan opened the door, letting an icy draft in with him.

"We got that doe," he said to Thorn. Irina let out a groan.

Seylin followed the elves outside into the frost and found his little doe, dead. Rowan and Willow had already tied her feet up to the tree branch, and Sable was capably gutting her into a tub. Seylin struggled against his feelings of horror and sadness. That poor little mother, carrying her unborn fawn!

"Good work," said the blond elf to the two hunters. "We're eating well this winter. Get over here, Irina," he barked as the petite elf girl came slouching up.

"Oh, Thorn, do I have to?" she whined. "Why is it always me?" Seylin noticed that it was always Sable, too, but the scarred woman knew not to argue.

"I'll help, Irina," said Seylin. Thorn shot him an irritated glance as he walked away.

Seylin didn't know what to do, so Sable had to tell him, and that made Irina giggle. She couldn't imagine not knowing how to butcher. She'd been doing it her whole life.

"I guess you weren't ugly where you came from, either," she concluded. "I wish you were. Then I wouldn't have to butcher anymore, or haul the kindling, or burn the bones, or empty out the guts tub. We always have to do that kind of stuff because we're the ugliest."

Seylin studied her bright, pretty face, her green eyes and golden, if dirty, hair. "Irina, what's wrong with how you look?" he asked. "What's ugly about you?"

Irina's face clouded over with the unaccustomed effort of thought.

"Oh, you know," she said vaguely, "ugliness. But, anyway, I'm not as ugly as her." She gestured at Sable, who rolled her eyes and kept cutting. This reminded him that he needed to talk to her.

"Sable, why did you ask me about goblins?" he demanded. The black-haired elf paused.

"That's what happened to the woman you loved," she said shortly. "You lost her to a goblin. Your band was doing well, and then the goblins came. It's the only thing that makes sense."

Seylin was stunned by the conjecture. He couldn't deny it. Marak was right: he certainly wasn't fooling her.

"You need to leave," begged the scarred woman. "You must have seen the goblins, but you don't know what they're like. They'll follow you and find us. They'll capture Irina and me, and we'll die down there with them. They use elf women to make monsters. They—they breed them to monsters, to make more. I'm sorry about the woman you loved. What a horrible way to die."

Seylin looked down at the meat he was cutting, thinking of the woman he loved. Emily had endless fun with her monster babies. A few weeks before he left, she'd been babysitting Bony's twins. The two boys had ram's horns, and they kept butting heads. The little boys running at each other had looked so hilarious that Emily had laughed till she cried. Sable's information about elf women and monsters was technically correct, but it wasn't anything like the goblin life he knew.

"Seylin, please leave," she urged, "before it's too late for Irina and me. Oh, I know, you think we don't have much of a life, but it's a good life, really. We're free."

"Sure, it is," grumbled Irina. "I just love my life." She hacked savagely at the shoulder, carving out strips. "My dress stinks of blood, and my hair's all greasy, and I can't even take a bath."

"Don't be absurd!" replied Sable. "Think what it would be like if the goblins came. We still have stars. We can look up and see the sky."

"Nice for you," retorted the blond girl. "I don't have time to look up. I've got all that cloth to weave because Thorn's in a hurry for his new cloak. What's stars got to do with it, anyway?"

"Goblins live underground," explained Seylin. "They live in what you'd call large caves."

"Oh," said Irina, absorbing this. She pulled her thin cloak around herself, leaving a bloody handprint on it, and glanced longingly at her own cave. "Are the goblin caves warm?" she asked wistfully.

"Irina, think!" cried Sable. "Don't you understand? You'd be bred to monsters, to die having a monster child!"

Seylin opened his mouth to protest this, but Irina cut him off.

"I would not," she stated complacently. "I'm not old enough to be married."

"Fine," said Sable sarcastically, "for another six months! Irina, you're so stupid!"

Irina just smiled. That was what they always said when she won an argument.

❧

"Em, think! Consider others for once in your life! Stop being so selfish!"

The two women and three children had been making their way

steadily toward home, moving from one wayside inn to the next at a comfortable pace. The weather was worsening, and Ruby insisted that the children should be safe in the kingdom, but Emily doggedly refused to give up her quest.

"Take them home if you want," she declared. "I'm staying outside."

"You know I can't do that. Marak assigned me to guard you."

The door opened, and a very wet Jack scampered in, wrapped up in a towel. "We're ready to get out," he announced, hopping up and down. Ruby caught him in her arms and began drying his hair.

"You stay in there by the fire," she ordered. "I'll be there in a minute."

"What's a minute?" demanded the little boy.

It never ceased to amaze Emily that the twins were so trusting and affectionate with the old gargoyle. They clung to the teacher like burrs. No child in the goblin kingdom would do such a thing. They all knew about Lore-Master Ruby.

"You'd better do what she says," she warned Jack. "If you don't, she'll make your tongue a foot long, and it won't fit in your mouth anymore."

The boy looked shocked at this, but Ruby just patted his head.

"That's ridiculous," she told him calmly. "Run along now and wait for me." Regaining his confidence, he dashed through the door. They heard a loud splash as it closed.

Ruby immediately turned and gave Emily a glare that could have blistered skin. "How *dare* you!" she hissed. "You're trying to frighten those little children!"

"I am not," protested the young woman, looking blank. "You work that spell all the time!"

"I wouldn't do such a thing to a poor little orphan."

Emily jumped to her feet, her patience at an end.

"You did it to me more times than I could count! And I'm an orphan, too!"

"You!" scoffed the ugly old teacher, turning to the door. "You've never suffered a day in your life. You've never been a thing like these children."

Emily gritted her teeth as the door slammed, her face on fire. Then she grabbed her cloak and marched from the room.

Outside, snow was falling softly in a quiet night. There was almost no wind at all. Richard had gone to the stable yard to eat a bag of nuts after Ruby had pointed out the mess he was making with the shells. He looked up at Emily's furious expression and cracked a walnut with a rock.

"What are you and the lady fighting about this time?" he asked cheerfully, holding out the nutmeat.

"She's not a lady," growled Emily, taking it, "and I wish you'd stop calling her that."

"Sure she is," replied the young goblin, "as you'd know if you'd seen as many of 'em as I have. There's women and ladies, let me tell you, and they're hardly the same thing. It's their respectability that makes the difference. You can see it with half an eye." He cracked a nut between his teeth and spit out the shell.

Emily thought about this as she took a nut from his bag. "My sister's a lady," she reflected. "I'm not," she added with a sigh.

"But you're fun," said Richard generously, "and that's saying something. You're an enlightening person to be around."

Emily smiled to herself. Although he had had no schooling, Richard loved big words, and she enjoyed listening to the creative uses he found for his ambitious vocabulary.

"Ruby says I wasn't ever like you and the twins, that I never had a hard day. But that's not true. I'm an orphan just like you are."

"Well, now, I don't know that you could really call me an

orphan," objected the goblin, "since I never had a mum or dad to lose. Mr. Simmons raised me, and a fine job he did. He took care of me right along."

"I thought you'd always been in the streets," remarked Emily. "Did this Mr. Simmons take you into his house?"

"Took me into his van, was more like it," asserted the boy. "Traveled with me the length and breadth of this isle. Showed me off in every little hamlet along the way, at a copper a peek or tuppence for the family."

"You mean he turned you into a sideshow?" demanded the astonished young woman.

"The one-and-only Devil Boy," announced Richard with gusto, smacking open another nut. "The only authenticated Fiend from Hell ever to be kept in captivity. With fangs, claws, and horns— that's my ears—and a cow's tail sewed in my trousers. We'd park, and he'd drum up a crowd and then pull back the curtain, and I'd be in a cage, clutching at the bars and snarling. For the grand finale, he'd launch into a church hymn, and I'd screech and fall into a faint. We did it right, let me tell you. He was a most assiduous showman."

"But—I mean—was he kind to you? You said he took care of you. Did he?"

"That he did," replied the boy good-naturedly. "He made sure I understood my part. Kept me down to one meal a day, but it was all for the good of the act. 'Richard, my boy,' he'd say while he was tucking into a leg of mutton, 'me old heart bleeds to keep this from you, but no one ever paid their brass to see a well-fed Devil Boy. Skin and bones, that's what they come to see, and we got to give them what they want.' He was laborious, was Mr. Simmons, most laborious indeed."

"And he made you sleep in a cage?" exclaimed Emily in disgust.

"'Course not!" Richard laughed. "No, the cage was just for the act. At night, he locked me up in a box so no one could steal a peek at me. Evenings, I'd sweep the van and tend the fire while he'd take a pull at a bottle and tell tales about his missus that ran off with a fortune-teller. We were amiable together, the two of us, and life was benevolent."

"Then why'd you leave?" Emily wanted to know.

"I didn't. The lads broke in and stole my box on a bet. When they got back to their place and let me out, they fell on the ground laughing. They made me the lucky-touch of the gang. It was the lads that taught me to pick pockets, to lift the nose-wipes and wallets and such. Didn't we have some jolly times! Didn't we just! But two of their best were pulled and tucked up proper. Put in lavender— hanged," he added at Emily's baffled expression.

"The lads said I'd turned their luck, and they drove me away. That's the lowest I ever was. I thought I might as well do myself in. But that's when I found my family, and I've been in charge of 'em ever since. Though it's nice to see the lady taking such good care of 'em now," he confided. "It's hard work raising a family."

Emily thought about being a child on the streets and looking after two hungry babies. Ruby had spoken the truth. Emily had never been what they were.

"I suppose I should let her take you home, where you'll all be safe," she admitted. "It is the unselfish thing to do. But I just hate to give up like this."

Richard nodded wisely. He'd heard all about Seylin, elf-hunter and erstwhile member of the King's Guard.

"You're wanting to follow your soldier," he said. "I don't blame you a bit."

Emily sighed. "I just wish I knew what Marak wanted me to do."

"I wouldn't let a king's ideas make up your mind," counseled the boy. "You do what you think best, and I'll back you against anybody.

Kings never would have cared for me, let me tell you. If they'd caught me, they'd have made me dance at the end of a rope."

He held up a nut and tried out the newly learned Fire Spell on it. When it burst into flames, he dropped it into the snow.

"What's he like, anyway, the ugly people's King?" he asked with pensive curiosity.

Even Emily's glib tongue and fertile imagination balked at the impossible task of describing Marak.

"He's a good King," she mused, trying to think of what to say. "He's fair, and he hardly ever stays angry very long. He's married to my sister," she added parenthetically. Richard's pale golden eyes almost popped out of his head.

"A King and your sister!" he exclaimed. "That makes you royalty, doesn't it!"

Emily grinned. "You could say that my life has been pretty benevolent," she replied.

The argument continued the next day in the carriage. They weren't very far from the goblin kingdom now, and the weather was awful. Ruby kept the carriage as tightly sealed as possible, but it was still very cold. She stayed in her regular form so that she could hold the twins close and keep them warm.

"We'll be home tomorrow if we travel through the night," she pointed out. "Em, I expect you to do the right thing for these little ones."

"But she wants to follow her soldier," protested Richard.

"Stop encouraging her," the teacher ordered him firmly. "The King commanded us goblins not to interfere in Seylin's work, so I'll thank you to be a good goblin and not interfere."

"I've got nothing against kings—live and let live, that's my plan—but I've never let their orders worry me."

"You wait until Marak gets his hands on you," declared Ruby. "You'll be singing a different tune then."

The goblin boy turned pale at these words and stared despondently at his boots. "I've said I'll back her, and I'll back her," was all he would answer. "No king has a hand on me yet."

Emily didn't speak. She thought about the elf girl's book in their pack and Marak Whiteye's betrayal of his mother's dreams, about their unexpected discovery in London and Ruby's growing fondness for the little humans. The quest hadn't been a failure. They had found some valuable things. But they hadn't found what Emily really wanted.

"Marak knew I was hunting for Seylin when he let me out," she said slowly. "He told me I would find what he wanted me to find."

"And you haven't found one hint about where Seylin is," observed Ruby. "Not in this whole long time."

"That's true," agreed Emily, her heart sinking. "Maybe Marak doesn't want me to find him. But you don't know, Ruby. Maybe he does. He could have just made me stay in the kingdom."

"How long are you going to drag us around while you try to make up your mind? I hardly call that responsible behavior."

The carriage stopped. They were changing horses. Emily leaned forward and lifted the leather flap over the window to peek at the village outside.

"You're right, Ruby," she said, amazed to hear herself say the words. The old goblin was amazed to hear them, too.

"So you think I'm right," she remarked suspiciously. "Right about what?"

"That it would be irresponsible to drag you around. I know Marak wouldn't want that. And I think—or, rather, I know—that it's about time I did something Marak wanted. He's been like a father to me, and I can't say that I've done much in return."

"Then you'll come back to the kingdom," declared Ruby triumphantly.

Emily hesitated.

"I'm just going to do one more thing," she said. "I'll ask in this town about Seylin, and if I don't learn anything, I'll give up. It won't take any time. We're stopped for a few minutes anyway."

"I'm coming with you," asserted the teacher. "I'm not falling for one of your tricks."

Emily stood on the frozen ruts of the little road, struggling against tears. A man passed them, leading their tired team to the stable.

"Ask him," whispered the squirrel on her shoulder.

"No, not him," she answered. "I'll just go a little farther." I don't know why, she thought. This is completely hopeless. Seylin, why didn't I listen when you came to talk to me? How could I just send you away?

The door of the inn opened, and a girl came out. She was warmly dressed, and her fair hair was held neatly in a large blue bow. She looks happy, thought Emily forlornly. She looks like I used to look. As the girl passed by, she glanced over and gave Emily a friendly smile.

"Excuse me," said Emily. "Have you seen a young man here in the last several months, very handsome, with black hair and dark eyes? Or wait—maybe you would have seen a very large, furry black cat instead."

The girl stopped and stared in surprise. Then she impulsively seized Emily's hand.

"You must mean Seylin!" cried Jane in delight. "Tell me, can your squirrel talk?"

Chapter Ten

During the morning meal, Sable kept trying to catch Irina's eye, but the blond girl wasn't paying attention. Irina was dwelling on the unhappy fact that Thorn always gave her less food now than Sable had given her in the past. She knew he'd always handed Sable her food, but she didn't see why he had to pick on her. Irina glanced up to find the black-haired woman once again looking at her significantly.

"What do you want?" she burst out. Everyone shifted to stare at her and then at the dismayed Sable. "Oh!" Irina added in a tone of discovery. "I remember now! Thorn, the ugly woman wanted me to remind you that the flour stores are running low."

Sable certainly hadn't intended the reminder to come out like this. Thorn turned, eyes narrowed, to study his dead wife, but Sable had such a look of surprised alarm on her face that he couldn't help laughing at it.

"Well, now you can do something for me, puppy," he said. "I want you to remind the ugly woman that I don't need her help running this camp. You tell her I already knew about the low stores. I've been waiting till we had enough food laid by to take the men out hauling flour." He turned to Rowan. "If the weather's not too bad, tomorrow night should be a good time. We'll go south this year. We haven't been that direction in a while. Last spring, I saw a place that might serve us well. It looked like they should have something."

The next night, the four men of the band set out to haul flour. Seylin wondered just exactly what this would mean. Normally, under the elf Kings, the elves had bought their flour from a nearby mill. They didn't bring grain, not having their own fields, but they sent representatives to place an order and then bring home the flour in sacks. This was one of only a few situations that required elves to interact with humans, and it was also one of the few that required money. Seylin wondered considerably about money as they walked along. He'd never met anyone less likely to have it.

They came to a comfortable farmhouse at some distance from a village. Candlelight shone through one window, and Thorn and Rowan crept up and squinted at the room that lay within. Then Thorn beckoned, and the company went to the low door. It wasn't locked. Thorn opened it, and they walked right in.

A smoky, rustic kitchen lay before them, with onions, herbs, and dried sausages hanging from the rafters. A small fire crackled on the grate, and an old farmer sat alone at the kitchen table, drinking a mug of beer. He rose at their intrusion.

"Now then," he said with wary dignity.

"Soft without but fierce within, live in caves like goblin kin," chanted Thorn. Seylin looked at him in amazement. He was speaking elvish, and his accent was terrible. Seylin glanced back at the farmer. The old man was gone. Before he realized what had happened, a white rabbit scurried across the table, heading for the door.

"Oh, for pity's sake!" exclaimed Seylin. "You didn't have to do that!" He looked through the door, trying to remember the counter-charm, but the rabbit was already gone.

"Yeah, I know," grunted Thorn, walking to the fire. "We could have handled him easily, but why dirty our hands with human trash?" He surveyed Seylin with a conceited look on his face. "You thought you were the only one who knew magic," he gloated.

"Thorn always changes humans into rabbits," explained Willow proudly, "and we can tell his when we hunt because they're white, not brown." Rowan was busy opening doors and looking through them. Hauling flour, Seylin realized, was nothing more than stealing from the neighbors.

"What about the other people who live here and just aren't home?" he demanded. "If you take their flour away, how are they supposed to live through the winter?" Thorn shrugged without interest. Willow cut down a sausage and sniffed at it.

"Hey!" said Thorn sharply. "Get rid of that thing. You know human food's not fit to eat." Willow obediently threw the sausage into the fire.

"Three good-sized bags," called Rowan from another room. "One's been opened, but not much is missing."

"Great!" said Thorn briskly, going to see. Willow stayed behind. Now he was sniffing the beer. Seylin eyed the boy gloomily. Willow was growing into a very handsome elf, with all the grace and dignity of his ancestors, and here he was stalking around a farmer's kitchen sniffing foods like a tame bear.

Rowan and Thorn struggled through the narrow pantry doorway, dragging a large bag of flour between them. They dropped it onto the neatly swept boards by the open door through which the rabbit had recently left.

"Don't just stand there," demanded Thorn, beckoning to Seylin. "Grab a bag!"

Dark eyes flashing, Seylin walked haughtily to the pantry and levitated the two remaining bags, floating them over to the door. He turned back to the fire, and the bags dropped with a thud. Rowan grinned at Thorn.

"Well, aren't we fine," he said with a laugh, but Thorn didn't look amused.

Willow appeared in a doorway, wearing a thick coat. "Look at this!" he said in excitement, rubbing the lapels between his fingers to feel how soft the cloth was.

"No, thanks," said Thorn. "Willow, get that thing off."

"Aw, Thorn, why?" demanded the boy miserably. "It's really warm."

Rowan walked by him into the room. "It's the wrong color," he explained. Willow glanced down. The coat was black. His winter cloak was brown.

"I won't say it again," threatened Thorn. "Do you want to look like a human?" The elf boy sighed and pulled off the coat, stroking its soft wool unhappily.

"Humans have all the luck," he muttered.

Rowan walked back into the room, holding a hand mirror.

"Irina might like this," he suggested, handing it to Thorn. Willow came to gawk at it. He could barely remember seeing a mirror. Thorn had thrown out their last fragment after Sable had used it when she cut her face.

"That's just what we need," growled Thorn, "Irina sitting around making faces at herself all night."

"Suit yourself," said Rowan with a shrug. "She's going to be your wife."

"She is?" whooped Willow. "You're joking! Wait'll I tell her!"

Thorn looked up, his gray eyes stern. "It's my business, Willow," he said steadily, "and you'll keep your nose out of it."

"Well," said the elf boy uncertainly, "don't you even want her to know?"

"No," snapped Thorn. "And I'll tell you why. The minute she knows, she'll start expecting handouts, pats on the back, chucks under the chin. You go that way with a woman, and she thinks she's the piper and you're the one to dance. You take it from me, Willow," he concluded, shaking the hand mirror at the boy. "Never be nice to a woman."

Willow considered this piece of advice. "I'm not nice to Irina," he pointed out. He followed the elf leader toward the door.

Seylin hung back while the other elves left the kitchen, considering what to do. The loss of the family patriarch as well as all the flour was bound to be a devastating blow. He took his remaining money from his pocket and put it all down on the table. The next time he needed money, he'd just have to do what everyone else did: work for it.

He followed Thorn to the barnyard. A big horse came stepping out of the barn to greet them, blowing softly, ears pricked with interest. His winter coat was dull and shaggy. He was a bit of a mongrel, with legs that were too short and fine for his deep barrel chest, but his eyes were lively and intelligent.

"Oh, good, a horse!" exulted Thorn. So they were going to steal a valuable animal as well as vital winter stores.

"We don't need the horse," protested Seylin. "I can float the bags home with the Carrying Spell."

"Fine," said Thorn, "and while you're at it, you can float home the horse, too. Look at the meat on him!" he said admiringly.

Seylin's jaw dropped. "You don't mean you're going to butcher this horse!" he exclaimed.

Rowan grinned at his shocked face. "Uh-oh!" he teased. "Thorn, he's a picky eater!"

Thorn didn't answer. He vaulted over the fence and headed into the barn.

"Horse is good," Willow assured Seylin. "It tastes kind of like deer." He and Rowan climbed over the fence as well. Seylin opened the gate and walked in after them. The horse followed him, breathing on the back of his neck.

"Wool," said Thorn. "Look up there." Rowan went up the

ladder into the loft, and after a minute, a bundle came hurtling down.

Seylin poked around the barn in search of food for the horse. He found oats and began shoveling them into a small sack. He thought moodily about the stables back in the goblin kingdom. Fine horses lived there. Marak was fond of horses, and so was Emily. So was he, for that matter. Living in the deep forest, elves normally had no use for horses and distrusted them accordingly, but he'd never read about any elves eating one before.

A noise distracted him. He came out of the barn to find his three companions chasing the horse around the barnyard, trying in vain to hoist a sack of flour onto his back.

"Stop it!" shouted Seylin. "Don't you people know anything about horses?"

"Of course we do," said Rowan with a laugh. "We know how to cook them."

They were home shortly before the morning meal. Sable and Irina had taken advantage of the men's absence to bathe and wash their clothes. Properly washed, Irina's blond hair was a mass of soft curls, and she was very happy and bubbly, chattering away and asking Willow about where they had gone. Willow was explaining about the sausage and the coat, forgetting for the moment his moral obligation not to be nice to women.

Even Sable's blue eyes were shining. She was clean, and she had had the luxury of combing out her black hair in peace. It looked like a crow's wing or a piece of black satin. Thorn noticed it, and his face took on a dangerous expression.

"Didn't you bring home anything besides horse and wool and flour?" demanded Irina. "Didn't you bring home anything fun?"

"No," said Willow with arrogant superiority. "Human trash isn't for elves."

"Oh, yes, we did," corrected Thorn, warming his hands before the fire. "We brought something else home."

"Did you? Thorn! What is it?" asked Irina, terribly excited.

"It's something just for elf women," said Thorn.

"Something for elf women?" echoed Irina, thrilled. But Thorn didn't look at her eager face. Instead, he looked down at his dead wife and her beautiful black hair.

"It's something Sable's been especially interested in," he continued. "Sable, with her sable hair." The scarred woman stood up to face him, thoroughly alarmed. He never used her real name anymore.

"Don't you want to know what it is, Sable?" he asked. She eyed him anxiously. There wasn't a right answer. Everyone was staring at her, and she flashed a nervous glance at them all. Thorn reached under his cloak.

"It's a goblin!" he shouted, holding up the mirror, and Sable cried out at the sight of herself. She threw up a hand to slap him, but she stopped herself in time and stood there gasping, her hands balled into fists.

Everyone laughed at her, even Irina, her pretty voice joining the rest. Everyone except Seylin, who looked at her mortified expression and felt thoroughly ill. Thorn stopped laughing. He took a step toward her, his gray eyes deadly.

"Now you know what it's like for the rest of us," he hissed. "We have to look at it every single night."

Seylin walked up to the elf leader, absolutely furious. "I'm leaving tomorrow," he said coldly.

Thorn turned toward him in surprise, and Sable made her escape.

"Leaving the camp, eh?" asked the blond elf without much interest. "I guess you finally believe me about the girl. Tomorrow's a good time for you, but not a good time for us. We'll be working all night butchering that monster outside. I expected you to do your share."

Seylin glared at the hateful elf.

"All right," he said shortly. "I'll help with the butchering, but I'm leaving the minute it's done."

Thorn shrugged. "Go right ahead," he said, turning away. He looked for Sable, but she was gone. "The ugly woman left her look-ing glass behind," he announced in mock concern. "Here, puppy, you might as well keep it."

"Oh, Thorn!" gasped Irina. She took the mirror from him, unable to believe her good fortune. It was terribly hard to admire a reflection in the water. Her hair always dragged into it and spoiled the view.

Sable came back to serve the morning meal. Thorn gave her no food. He ate heartily, tipping up the bowl to slurp the last of the stew. He wiped his dirty hands and face on his remaining bread as if it were a dinner napkin. Then he flipped it through the air so that it fell in the dirt at Sable's feet.

Don't pick it up, thought Seylin. Don't give him the satisfaction of watching you eat it. But the scarred woman snatched the dirty bread and dusted it off hurriedly. Such a large piece. Who would have thought he would give her so much? And she devoured it in quick bites before he could change his mind.

✥

"Em, this is madness," said Ruby. "He left months ago." But Emily wasn't listening.

"We were right here," noted Jane, leading the way into the snowy clearing. "This is where he worked his magic. He told me not to tell anyone," she added to Emily, "but I don't think he'd have minded this, do you?"

"I hope not," said Emily, looking around.

"I won't tell," volunteered Richard.

"What magic did he work?" asked Ruby, studying the clear sky. The stars were shining very brightly.

"He changed the constellations into wonderful shapes, like harps and wreaths and thrones. He made a flower bush out of light. He wrote my name in sparks. He made the rabbits come out of their holes and— Good heavens! What's that?!"

A large white rabbit came crashing out of the frozen underbrush and collided with Jane's legs. Then it curled up on top of her feet and sat there, shivering.

"Do you think I did that?" she wondered, turning to the group. "Did Seylin give me the power to call rabbits?"

Ruby knelt down and examined the terrified beast. "That's not a rabbit," she replied.

Minutes later, an old farmer huddled in the snow, talking to himself, while the rest of them stood around and watched him. "'Now then,' I said. 'Now, then. What's all this?' And then I was all over fur! Thanks, missus," he added as Ruby handed him a flask. "Lord, you're ugly to be an angel."

"Do you think it was a sorcerer who did it?" Emily wanted to know. The teacher shook her head.

"That's an elvish spell," she pointed out. "It makes a very pretty rabbit."

"Rabbit!" exclaimed the old man distractedly. "That's what they made of me. A rabbit! All that blessed fur! Where's my home? If this is heaven, I don't like it one bit. It's cold and soggy."

Emily sat down next to the farmer.

"Did you see elves?" she asked eagerly. "Was one of them good-looking? Well, I suppose all elves are good-looking—but did one have black hair and black eyes?"

"They attacked me!" blurted out the man. "Busted right into my kitchen! Elves? How should I know? They murdered me! And then I was a rabbit!"

They finally got the old man onto his feet and brought him to Jane's house, where she and her father discussed local events until the farmer gave up the idea of being in heaven. His village, it turned out, was not far away. Jane stayed home with the sleepy twins while her father drove the rest of them to the farmer's house in a wagon.

"Seylin saved Jane from the smallpox," he told them, "and he really saved my life, too. I had never realized how much she meant to me until I thought I was going to lose her. For the first time since her mother died, I'm not just living in the past."

They arrived at the farmer's cottage.

"I can't interfere," Ruby told Emily. "Not if elves are in the house." But the elves were gone, and so was the farmer's horse and all his flour. In their place was a small pile of money on the kitchen table. Emily called Ruby in to look at it.

"That's Seylin's money," she pointed out. "Dwarf-made coins. He must have been with the intruders and paid for the things they took. I can't go back to the kingdom now. He's nearby, and I have to find him."

The goblin woman sat down at the table to examine the little hoard. "But the children!" she insisted in dismay.

Jane's father had been helping the distraught old man to bed. He came back into the room in time to hear Ruby's comment.

"The twins can stay with us for a while," he offered. "Jane and I can look after them."

"And I want to help Em find her soldier," noted Richard.

"I can't allow that," replied Ruby. "Marak has word of you children, and he wants to see you right away. And, Em, I have to be the one to take the twins to him. Marak won't mind Martha, but he won't want Jack in the kingdom. There's a law against having an elf or human man ever live down there with us. But I've been thinking. If the right person promised to look after them in a quiet place across the lake valley, maybe the King would let them stay until Jack grows up. I have to be there to ask Marak about it before he makes up his mind."

Emily was astounded.

"The right person? Ruby, you can't mean you! You're going to volunteer to raise humans? What about teaching the pages?"

"I'm tired of teaching. I want a change. You were right, I made everyone hate my class. And you know what it's like to be a human," said the old woman appealingly. "I can't bear for those children to grow up without help."

Emily sat down on the bench next to her. "I think that's a good plan," she said generously. "I think they need you. Go home with them, Ruby. I'll be fine on my own."

"I can't allow that, either." Ruby shook her head emphatically. "The King insisted that you were always to have a goblin nearby to guard you."

"Well, I'm a goblin, aren't I?" pointed out young Richard. "I can do that Fire Spell about as well as you can. And I'm not so anxious to meet this ugly King. I'd rather stay here and help Em."

Ruby started to speak, but Emily spoke before she could answer.

"We aren't far from Seylin now, and we aren't far from home," she said. "If we don't find him quickly, I'll bring Richard to the kingdom myself. Marak won't mind. He'll know you did everything he told you to do."

They walked out into the frosty night, and Jane's father climbed up onto his wagon. Ruby started to follow him, but then she turned back.

"Goodbye, Em," she said. "You and Richard be careful. And"—she hesitated for a second—"and I hope you find Seylin."

"You do?" demanded Emily, more shocked than before. The old goblin looked embarrassed.

"For his sake, really, if he wants to marry you," she muttered. "He was always such a good boy."

Emily stared at her nemesis, remembering their countless class-room battles. It was strange to think that she'd never realized what a brat she had been. She knew Ruby hadn't been fair about humans back then, but she'd never helped the goblin understand them, either. She supposed if she'd been Ruby she would have murdered a student like her.

"Ruby, there's something I need to tell you," she said slowly. "All those tests—all those perfect scores—"

The teacher stiffened, and her white eyes narrowed in an angry glare.

"I studied and studied to earn them," Emily admitted in a rush. "I did all the homework, too, but I made sure no one ever found out. I studied more for your class than I did for any of the others. It was such hard work it almost killed me."

Ruby's lipless mouth broke into a smile so wide that it seemed it would split her face in two. But when she spoke, it wasn't to Emily. Instead, she crooked a finger at Richard.

"Come here, you smart little goblin," she told the street urchin. "I'm going to teach you another spell. This one tracks things and shows you where they went. Why don't you practice it on those foot-prints over there?"

chapter Eleven

The next night, Seylin was up early. He struck his tent and packed his belongings, fuming to himself. He couldn't wait to go, but he was furious that he should have to. These were his people. They should have welcomed him. And even if they were ignorant and savage, they didn't have to be awful. They were fools and bullies, and the only intelligent member of the band just wanted him to leave.

He went outside to feed the horse, and his heart sank at the sight of the friendly animal. He stroked the horse's rough coat and rubbed his broad forehead. Those dark eyes watched him willingly. What are we going to do now? they asked. You're going to become a steaming carcass, thought Seylin unhappily. And once you're bloody bones and parts, I can leave this horrid place.

Rowan came through the door, testing the new edge he had put on his metal knife. Only Thorn had a real elf knife like Seylin's.

"What are you doing?" Rowan grinned. "Playing with your food?"

"I'm not eating this horse," replied Seylin with dignity.

"Oh, that's right," said Rowan, sobering up. "You're leaving. Good luck finding an elf woman."

Thorn came outside and began to issue orders. The women built a fire in the yard and began rearranging the meat in the shed. The shed was filling up, and Sable was considering where to put tonight's butchering. Seylin glanced into the shed and was sorry he did. He wouldn't have shared their meals if he'd seen it.

He went back to the men and discovered that they had a problem. It seemed that butchering the horse wasn't nearly as big a chore as killing it. Untrained in magic, they lacked the power to fell a big animal.

"Rowan, you do it," said Thorn. "Your Hunting Spell works better than mine or Willow's." But Rowan didn't look pleased at the compliment.

"Oh, no," he said firmly. "Not after what happened last time."

Willow made a face. "Was that disgusting!" he said. "And then we still had to whack it to death with a stick."

"Then we'll start there this time," decided Thorn. "Willow, go get a log from the woodpile." The elf boy obediently went off and returned with a decent-looking club. "Now whack him with it," directed their leader.

"What, me?" asked the boy, his face a picture of distress. "Why do I have to do it?"

"Because I'll whack *you* if you don't," threatened Thorn.

But Willow didn't make any move toward the horse. To him, it wasn't a friendly servant. It was a huge, frightening beast with four sharp hooves and big teeth. Thorn watched him with a thoughtful frown.

"Rowan, maybe you and I could work killing spells at the same time while Willow hits it with the log," he said.

"And maybe we could manage to kill Willow that way," replied Rowan. He turned, his eyes bright, and patted Seylin on the shoulder. "I know who can kill our dinner for us," he suggested. "He knows all about horses." Seylin just frowned at him. He'd been expecting this.

"Seylin, you kill it, then," directed Thorn, "if you really think you can do it."

Seylin crossed his arms and studied the animal. He liked the horse, and it wasn't going to be his food, but he knew how to kill it humanely, and he couldn't leave until it was butchered. He sighed and stretched out his hand.

"Don't you dare! You kill that horse and I'll never speak to you again as long as I live!" Seylin froze in complete astonishment. It wasn't—no, it couldn't be—

"A human!" shouted Willow, and they all turned to look. Emily stood up from behind a large rock. She was pale and grubby, and she had circles under her eyes. Seylin had never seen a sight more beautiful.

"Em!" he cried. "What are you doing here?"

Emily walked toward the group, her face uncertain.

"Seylin, I know that you had wanted—and I didn't— Well, I just came to say that if you'd rather marry one of these elves, I understand."

"He certainly wouldn't want to marry you," scoffed Irina. "You're so ugly."

Emily's uncertain manner fell from her. "Looks aren't everything," she snapped.

"Yes, they are!" insisted Irina hotly. "Aren't they?" she added in a puzzled tone, looking to her companions for support.

"Em," said Seylin, "what about Thaydar?" Of all the questions running around in his brain, this seemed the only one worth asking.

"Don't be absurd!" exclaimed his sweetheart. "After all the times we've quarreled, I can't believe you really thought I meant that!"

Seylin's world became a bright, shining, happy place. He walked over to her in a kind of dream.

"You're not married to Thaydar?" he asked. Emily just smiled at him, and Seylin's world reached perfection.

"You're going to marry a human?" exclaimed Willow in disgust. Seylin tore his eyes away from that smile to look at the boy.

"She has elf blood," he said loftily.

"Ugh! A half-breed," sneered Willow. Now Emily looked at him.

"I may be a half-breed," she said tartly, "but I'm not wearing my last eighteen meals on the front of my shirt." Irina gave a happy giggle.

"You ought to change her into a rabbit, Thorn," pointed out Willow, scowling fiercely. "You always do when they find our camp."

Thorn shrugged. "She's Seylin's business," he muttered. But Seylin had seen Sable's astounded face. He didn't want to wait around for questions.

"I'll get my pack," he told Emily. "We're leaving."

"Hey!" said Thorn indignantly. "What about the horse?"

"You want to eat him. Kill him yourself," replied Seylin, disappearing through the door.

Emily came up to the horse, glaring at the silent elves.

"And is it a nice horse?" she crooned, scratching him under the halter straps. "We don't want to be dinner for nasty elves, do we? Imagine eating a horse!" she exclaimed. "How disgusting!"

"Imagine marrying a half-breed," sneered Thorn. "How disgusting."

"I wouldn't marry you, either, you horse-eating bully!" cried Emily. "I'd slit my throat first."

"I'd help you," promised Thorn. He crossed his arms, very annoyed. He wanted to kill the horse now just to upset her, but Rowan had disappeared, and he didn't think Willow and he could do it alone. "You'd make a nice rabbit," he mused darkly, watching her stroke the horse.

"Look what I've found," called Rowan. He returned from the forest, dragging something with him, and Emily turned with a gasp.

"Richard!" she cried. Rowan had him by his white hair. The boy gave her an encouraging grin, and the elves blanched at the sight of his one fang.

"Good evening, sirs, ladies," said the boy, bowing as far as he could without losing hair and tugging at his forelock politely. Irina let out a shriek of revulsion, and Richard sighed resignedly. That always happened. But Sable came forward to look at him and let out a bloodcurdling scream.

"Thorn! He's a goblin! He's a goblin!" she screamed.

"Don't you touch him," shouted Emily, darting forward to try to loosen Rowan's hands, but he caught the neck of her cloak and held her off from the captured boy.

"You stay out of this," he advised.

Thorn held out his hand to begin his Rabbit Spell, but Sable clutched his arm in a frenzy of terror.

"Don't, Thorn, don't!" she begged. "There'll be more! They're always together, and you'll bring revenge if you hurt him. We can't fight, we have to leave now, we have to get away before the others come!" She caught his hand, risking life as a rabbit herself.

Thorn shoved her away, trying to concentrate on his rhyme, but Seylin ran up and reached out his own hand in a protection spell. A bubble formed in the air around the goblin child, wobbling in a shiny globe and prying Rowan's fingers free from his hair.

"Let them go, Rowan," he warned. "We'll just leave. We don't want a fight." He walked through the group, concentrating on the spell. Rowan released the two outsiders as Thorn struggled with the hysterical Sable.

They might have gotten safely away, but Willow looked down at that moment and realized he was still holding the club. As Seylin walked by him, he swung it up and hit Seylin over the head.

The bubble around Richard's body popped with a sigh, and Seylin fell unconscious to the ground. So did Rowan. So did Thorn. So did Willow. Grotesque shapes jumped from hiding and raced toward the group. Seylin's agreement with the goblin King was over.

chapter Twelve

Sable crouched on the ground by Thorn's side. She heard shouts, exclamations, Irina screaming frantically, and then her screams suddenly cut off. She saw the shadows of the newcomers pass to and fro on the snow around her, but she forced herself not to look up. It was the end of everything, the end of her life. She didn't want to see it.

Father was right, she thought. They all were right. I should have been safely dead long ago, and I wouldn't have had to live through this. Now I'll be tortured and used in horrible magic because I was cowardly and weak. A shadow fell across Thorn's quiet face and across the snow around them.

"Don't worry," said a good-natured voice, low and rich. "We didn't hurt him. He's just sleeping."

Sable went rigid. The voice was talking to her. She stared at the snowy ground, clinging to her life, her world. No one had grabbed her and dragged her away yet. She was still free.

"You gave him good advice," continued the voice thoughtfully. "He really should have listened to you." The voice was almost in her ear. A goblin, right behind her. Sable's nerve broke, and she abandoned her old life. She made a scramble for freedom, but an arm wrapped around her waist before she could even stand up.

"No, no," protested the voice, "you have to stay with me," and Sable was lifted off her feet by big silver-gray arms. The next thing she knew, she was carried up to that traitor elf, the one who had lied and brought the goblins here. He was struggling to sit up, his face very white, and some huge, strange form was doctoring the wound on his head.

"Sorry, Seylin," it said. "Orders. We had to let him hit you."

Sable looked away from that evil creature, its hideous striped face and gnarled hands. Look at the trees, she told herself. Look at the sky. Don't give them the pleasure of making you scream. The monster who held her knelt down on one knee and seated her on his other knee.

"Seylin," said the rumbling, good-natured voice. "Do you have a prior claim to this elf bride?"

Seylin turned away from Katoo's ministrations and caught sight of Sable staring out over his head as if he weren't even there.

"Oh, no!" he cried. "Oh, poor Sable! She's had a horrible life, Tinsel. Be nice to her."

"I will," promised Tinsel. "I'm always nice," he added with perfect truth. Seylin watched the handsome silver-haired goblin touch the elf woman's scarred cheek.

"Did that rabbit-lover hurt her?" he asked with an unaccustomed frown. Seylin flinched as Katoo rubbed the healing salve into his wound.

"No," he answered. "She did that herself so she wouldn't have to marry him."

"Makes sense to me," commented Tinsel. "I didn't care for him, either. But maybe you'll like me better. Right, Sable?"

Hearing her name, Sable slowly turned her head and looked up at the monster that had trapped her, at the wide chest draped in black, the broad metal-colored face, the hair glittering in the starlight like the forest after an ice storm. And, looking down at her, dark blue eyes just like her own. Elf eyes, captured and locked up in a goblin's face.

The big monster smiled down at her, and Sable's nerve broke again. She made a lunge to escape, but there wasn't the slightest chance of freedom. She mastered herself once more and froze, staring out at the trees, and Seylin could have cried at the expression on her face.

Thaydar came up, his arms full of unconscious Irina and his green cat-eyes gleaming with excitement.

"Seylin," he said, kneeling down and lowering his bundle, "do you have a prior claim to this elf bride? Marak said it would be best for the kingdom if his lieutenant married one of the captured elves. The importance of the position, that sort of thing," he explained modestly.

"But, Thaydar," protested Seylin angrily, "Marak promised me no raids for brides!"

"Oh, absolutely," agreed Thaydar. "We weren't dispatched for that at all, just to protect Em and her goblin escort and bring them safely back home. But Marak *did* say that if we didn't catch up to them in time to prevent their contacting you, *and* if you were to suffer any sort of harm in a fight, we should be prepared for the eventuality of taking brides, so he picked me for Irina and Tinsel for Sable.

"And, lo and behold," said Thaydar with a grin, "there did turn out to be a scuffle. Even if Richard hadn't provoked hostilities, Tinsel and I had thought up some nice ways to start a fight. A blast of snow in the face of the right elf as you walked by, or that horse's halter rope breaking, and him trotting off after you. Now, don't get upset," he added as Seylin started to speak. "We knew we weren't supposed to contact the elves. But a little snow's not really contact, is it? And some military commander I'd be if I couldn't bring home a couple of elf brides to my King."

Seylin surveyed the happy gleam in Thaydar's eyes. Marak was right: it was best for the kingdom that his lieutenant marry one of the brides. There was absolutely no way the clever Thaydar would go out on an errand of such personal and professional importance and come back to the kingdom empty-handed.

"Just look at her," gloated the fanged lieutenant, cradling the blond girl. "Isn't she the cutest thing you ever saw?"

"Thaydar," said Seylin irritably, "don't you think you ought to revive her?"

"Oh, I did," growled Thaydar cheerfully, "but she passed right out again. So now I think, best to let nature take its course, eh?" He beamed at the disheartened Seylin and walked off, carrying the insensible girl with him.

Sable was standing up now, and the monster was only holding her with one hand, but she still couldn't get away. He was doing something to her hand, some sort of magic, and she kept waiting for it to hurt. He was talking again, probably to her. Maybe she could learn some clue that would help her escape. She studied his moving lips, but she couldn't seem to hear him. His lips were metal-colored, too, and she wondered if they were cold like metal knives.

"Leash . . . ten feet . . . walk on your own . . ." he was saying. ". . . Would you like that better?" He stopped talking, and she stared at him, tense with fear.

"Sable, do you understand?" the monster asked. Yes, she understood. She was captured, trapped, she couldn't get away. He was still watching her, expecting some sort of answer. She cringed, afraid that he would yell at her, and nodded her head nervously.

"All right," he said a little doubtfully, and he released her hand and took a step back.

Sable felt giddy. She was free. It must be some sort of trick. She walked cautiously by him, expecting him to reach out and grab her, but he didn't. Two more steps, one more step, and she was out of reach. She made a dash for the nearby woods. Her hand flew back, and she whirled, off balance, caught by some invisible force. Then the force released her, and she fell facedown into the snow.

Stunned by the fall, Sable lay without moving. In another second, his hands were on her again. She closed her eyes tightly, expecting yelling, beating, a slap across the face. Sable didn't open her eyes as those hands lifted her out of the snow. She had been hit many times. She knew what was coming.

Dismayed, Tinsel picked up the unresisting elf woman and brushed the snow from her face.

"Are you all right?" he asked worriedly, using the Locating Spell. No injuries, but she sagged in his arms as if she had fainted. Tinsel carefully propped her up against a tree.

"Are you all right?" he asked again, deeply concerned.

Sable opened her eyes and winced at the sight of the monster's face, but those hands hadn't hit her yet, and that deep voice still wasn't yelling at her. "I'm so sorry," it was saying, quiet and worried. "I should have known you'd do that. If I were in your place, I suppose I'd have done it, too. We'll just sit here for a few minutes. You can rest until the others are ready to go."

"Come show us where this one belongs, Seylin," called Katoo as he and Brindle shuffled by, carrying the sleeping Willow between them. Seylin and Emily went into the cave, and Seylin pointed to Willow's tent. The two goblins slung the elf boy into it and pulled his cloak over him. Then they went back outside to get another elf.

"What a pigsty!" exclaimed Emily, looking around. She glanced back up to find Seylin looking at her and blushed unexpectedly. Seylin thought about how miserable he had been thinking she was someone else's wife. She had been right about his behaving like an old governess. He had acted self-important and priggish.

"I didn't like living with elves," he said. "I was a fool to leave."

"Hmm," said Emily noncommittally. "You weren't the only fool. Did you know I actually made my peace with Ruby?"

"With the old lore-master? You two?" Seylin laughed. "Em, you have to be lying."

"No." Emily's eyes danced. "For once, I'm not lying. And if you hate elves and I like Ruby, it must be the start of a new world."

"Our world," said Seylin. "Yours and mine." And he put his arms around her, drew her close, and kissed her.

Seylin retrieved his pack and brought it back into the cave.

"I want to leave Rowan my knife," he said, laying it beside the sleeping elf, "and I want to give Willow my spare cloak because his is just a rag," he added, remembering the poor boy's delight over a warm coat. Then he put his extra winter clothes in Rowan's tent and dumped out the summer clothes as well. They had so little, he reflected, and they wouldn't turn up their noses at his clothes, which were proper elf colors.

"You're not going to leave this poor horse here to be eaten, are you?" demanded Emily as they came out of the cave. "I don't see why you should. You paid for him."

"Of course not," Seylin assured her. "They have plenty of meat." He untied the horse from the tree and led him up to the group. "Now we just need to think of a good name for him."

"Let's call him Dinner," suggested Emily.

"We could load him up as a packhorse," proposed Katoo, but Brindle shook his head.

"Marak said the comfort of the brides comes first," he reminded them. "Thaydar, since your bride is too upset to walk, I'd recommend that you ride."

Irina had awoken shortly before and was shrieking and sobbing under Thaydar's fond gaze, making poor Dinner rather jittery. When they hoisted her up onto the horse, she took one look around and fainted again.

Sable stood silently, holding on to her composure with a supreme effort. How long, she wondered, before the goblin caves? Where were the others, and when would they start the torture? Were they like humans, who kept their animals in little cages until they were ready to enjoy the slaughter? Now the monster was talking to her again. "... keepsakes ... anything you want ... won't be coming back ..." He stopped talking and looked at her. She stared at him helplessly. What did he want her to do?

"I don't think she can understand me, Seylin," said Tinsel thoughtfully. "This has been too much of a shock. Do you know if there's anything she might want to take with her?" He looked at the elf woman doubtfully as he said this. If her stained and ragged clothes were typical of the rest of her possessions, they should all be burned as soon as possible.

"Sable! Your father's book!" exclaimed Seylin, and he went back into the cave and returned with the old camp chronicle. "I'll keep it for you. You can have it whenever you want."

They set off into the night, following Brindle's lead, and walked the hours away. They soon left the elves' little forest behind. Sable watched the half-moon rise. They were on a snowy trail along the ridge of a hill, and the white fields around them were completely bare of trees. She had never before left her network of groves, and the enormity of the landscape unsettled her. It allowed her to see more of the stars that were appearing and disappearing in the cloudy sky, but it made her feel very unsafe. Tinsel watched her frightened face and could imagine what she was thinking. He knew from his page classes that elves never left the cover of the trees.

"I know you'd rather be in the forest," he said to her in a low voice. "But we're going this way because we'll be home faster. We'll be in the kingdom the night after tomorrow night, and then we'll be married. I know you don't want to marry a goblin, but I'm not so bad."

Sable continued to stare at the fields as if she hadn't heard. She wished that she hadn't. Her shock was wearing off, and the fear that they were about to cause her horrible pain was slowly ebbing away, but the reality of her situation was becoming clearer. She was finding it harder to ignore the bizarre shapes of the goblins and the strange new landscapes that they were walking through. She couldn't help understanding now the things that they said. And, worst of all, she had come to realize that she wasn't being dragged off to be bred to monsters, but to this monster, the one that had her by the hand. It wasn't just, as Thorn had always said, a story to frighten children. It was true, and this monster kept talking about it.

So did the other monster, the one that held Irina on the horse. Poor Irina, she was so terrified. He looked simply frightful. He had two long white teeth at the corners of his mouth, and his eyes were like a cat's. His voice was loud and gravelly, and he boomed when he laughed. Sable winced, looking at him and at the other outlandish shapes, at the sharp teeth, the long ears, the claws, the big twisted bodies. Golden cat-eyes, green cat-eyes, dark orange eyes with no white to them, like a bird's. It could have been one of them holding her now. She shivered a little.

At least the goblin that held her hand was quiet, and he didn't look like they did. He was a strange color, but he had normal hands, normal teeth, and normal ears. She tilted her head to look up at him, and those blue elf-eyes looked down into hers. He smiled at her serious face, and she looked away again quickly.

Shaky from the shock and terribly tired, she watched her feet stepping and stepping into the snowy tracks made by the others. The monotony of the endless motion dragged on her low spirits, and she stumbled along, half asleep.

Irina had almost cried herself out. Earlier in the night, she had alternated between screaming and fainting, and the fainting had been a real relief for the poor girl. Later, she had alternated between shrieking and crying, but neither of them had proved as satisfactory as the fainting. Now she was sobbing rather listlessly. It was beginning to occur to her that none of the methods she had tried so far was really improving the situation.

"What are you crying about?" growled Thaydar cheerfully. "No one's hurting you. No one's being mean. What's the matter, anyway?"

"I don't like horses," sobbed Irina. "Not except to eat."

"Well, don't you worry," said Thaydar. "You can walk if you want to. And once we're home and married, you won't ever have to see another horse as long as you live."

"I don't want to marry you!" wailed Irina, rubbing her hand across her eyes. She was starting to see halos around everything, she had cried for so long.

"Sure, you do," answered Thaydar with such confidence that Irina felt confused. "Why wouldn't you want to marry me?"

"Because you look so scary," she sobbed.

"But that's good," Thaydar told her serenely. "I'm a goblin. We're supposed to look scary." Irina thought about this. She decided it was probably true. "Don't worry, you'll get used to me in no time, and then you won't think I'm scary anymore."

"Really?" asked Irina hopefully. She didn't like being scared. It had worn her out.

"Really," he growled. "Now, don't cry anymore. A beautiful girl like you shouldn't ever have anything to cry about." Irina gulped and looked up at the fanged goblin. He smiled broadly at her, but she didn't faint.

"You—you think I'm beautiful?" she sniffled in a tone of wonder.

"I think you're very beautiful," he assured her.

"Then I'm pretty?" she asked, wiping her runny nose on the back of her hand.

"You're the prettiest thing I ever saw," he declared firmly.

Irina sat up a little straighter and forgot to cry for a minute.

"Then I'm not ugly and clumsy?" she wanted to know.

"Anyone who calls you that," roared Thaydar, "should be pummeled and horsewhipped!"

Irina thought about Thorn and Willow being pummeled and horsewhipped and broke into a little giggle. Then she looked at her goblin champion with new eyes. He was so big and strong and scary, he could just about do it, too.

"Does that mean I won't have to do the butchering where we're going?" she asked in a tone of great discovery.

"A little thing like you, with her hands all covered with dead sheep?" boomed Thaydar. "You must be joking!"

"No, she's not joking," interrupted Seylin. "The men made Sable and Irina do all the butchering. They had a rule that the ugly people butchered, and they said that meant the two women."

The cat-eyed lieutenant looked at the charming girl he held and felt deeply and righteously indignant. "Well, not anymore!" he promised stoutly. "My wife won't do any butchering she doesn't want to do."

"Oh!" breathed Irina with shining eyes. Now, *that* was a good reason to be the scary goblin's wife.

"No wonder your dress is all covered with stains!" fumed Thaydar. "We'll get rid of it right away, and you'll have some nice clothes. Ten dresses, twelve, fourteen, as many as you want. I can't wait to see you in a nice green satin to match your eyes."

"But it's winter," protested Irina doubtfully. "Don't I have to wear brown?"

"You can wear any color you want," insisted the goblin. Irina's eyes grew large.

"Can I have a blue dress?" she whispered in awe. Elves never wore blue, but it was her favorite color.

"Of course you can have a blue dress," growled Thaydar, smiling at her.

"Can I—can I have a *red* dress?" she faltered. She knew elves would never, ever wear red, but when fresh blood spilled onto the snow, it was so rich and magnificent.

"You can have a red dress, too," promised her goblin warmly, and Irina was beside herself with delight. All her life, she had hated her coarse, ugly clothes. She looked up at those terrifying cat-eyes and gave Thaydar a happy smile.

"What about a yellow dress?" she wanted to know.

Thaydar was feeling a little beside himself, too. He'd sought Emily's hand in marriage for the honor of an elf-cross bride, and he'd left the kingdom intent on the honor of a pure elf bride. He had been terribly proud of the beauty of his hysterical captive, but when Irina smiled at him, with those lovely green eyes, those perfect white teeth, and that adorable little chin, his tough old soldier's heart just turned to mush. Thaydar's life was never the same again. Making Irina smile became one of the goals of his existence, starting from that moment.

"You can have five yellow dresses," he promised. It worked. She smiled again. "Make that ten." Her smile grew bigger.

"Now you're just being silly," she said. He was glad she could tell because he wasn't entirely sure. Emily grinned, listening to them, and Katoo and Brindle exchanged glances. Who would have thought, their eyes told each other, that the boss was such an idiot?

Sable roused herself to the dreary reality of slavery. She looked at the snowy barrenness around them, and a lump came into her throat. This treeless wasteland was as frightening as the goblins were. It made her situation even harder to endure. She stared at the path before her feet, listening dully to the crunch of the snow, the growl of the goblins' voices, the thump of the horse's hooves, and Irina. Poor Irina. Sable looked up with a start. Poor Irina was—laughing?

". . . and we'll have a little girl and a little boy," Thaydar was dreamily expounding for his giggling bride. "The little girl just as pretty as her mother is, and the little boy with fangs. And they'll be pages, and you'll go to court to see them serving their turn by the King's throne, all dressed up in their uniforms, and you'll just be so proud—"

"You'll be dead," interrupted a clear voice. Irina's face went pale. Thaydar turned, astounded at the intrusion. It was the other elf bride.

"What did you say?" he roared.

They stopped. All those animal eyes were staring at Sable now. She flinched and ducked her head nervously, but she was too upset not to speak.

"You'll be dead, Irina," she said, "with that very first baby. You'll die before you even see its face. We both will—you know that's just a woman's life. He's telling you a lie."

Irina began to sob, and Thaydar was furious. "Goblins never lie!" he thundered angrily, and Sable flinched again at the sight of those blazing eyes.

"She doesn't know that, Thaydar," observed Tinsel reasonably. "That must be some old scary tale the elf girls told each other about marrying goblins. It's not true, Sable. Having a goblin's baby isn't different from having an elf's baby."

Sable looked up at his friendly blue eyes with a little feeling of relief, but she was confused at his apparent sincerity.

"It doesn't matter whether the father's a goblin or an elf," she told him in a low voice. "That's just what happens when women have a child. Women have to die, that's how babies are born." Tinsel looked down at her sober face, puzzled as well.

"What a load of rubbish!" roared Thaydar. "Women survive childbirth every day." Sable winced at his loud voice and looked around nervously at all those strange eyes again.

"My wife's still alive after two," observed Brindle helpfully.

"I have both my grandmothers," added Katoo, his striped tabby face thoughtful. "And my mother's still alive, and she had quadruplets."

"But I think you cat folk are different," cautioned Brindle. "It's always quadruplets with you; that's not really normal."

Sable stared at the serious faces of the monsters, losing her confidence. Why would they try to talk her out of something so obvious? It must be a trick.

"Maybe goblin women aren't like that," she said. "Maybe just elf women are that way. But I know it's the truth. I know! I've seen the women die."

"She's right," said Seylin in the pause that followed. "Elf women are different from goblin women. They have a very hard time with childbirth, and they can't survive it without magic. I understand what happened now. Sable has the camp chronicle, and her great-great-grandfather's last entry told of a terrible accident. Almost all of the women were asphyxiated in one night. But the elf lord said that something even worse had happened, and now I know what it was. They lost the birthing magic. Only those dead women knew it. From that day on, the women in the camp were doomed to die in childbirth.

"I suppose they just told the little girls that that was the way life was," he conjectured. "And by the time Sable was born, they wouldn't have remembered anything different. Of course! That's why you didn't want to marry Thorn!" he said in a tone of discovery.

Sable drew her breath in sharply, feeling trapped by the revelation. Now all the monsters knew that she'd refused her marriage out of fear.

"But, Sable," he continued earnestly, "you don't have to worry about that anymore. We have entire books of elvish birthing magic. I can show them to you when we get home."

Sable glared at the elf. He called that torture chamber a home! And how dare he play on her weakness like that, trying to trick her now that he knew she was a coward!

"I don't want to learn anything from you, you traitor!" she hissed. "The goblins' tame elf, going out and finding them fresh blood. I begged you to leave so the goblins wouldn't come, and you promised me I was safe. You've never done anything but lie."

Seylin's face fell, and he looked away.

"That's not fair!" cried Emily. "He didn't know that we were coming!"

"It's all right, Em." He sighed. "She has a point."

"I don't think you could call Seylin a traitor," said Tinsel. "Both his parents are goblins." Sable stared at Seylin in horror and bewilderment. That handsome elf, a goblin's son? What other frightful things would they tell her, and how could she tell which were true? "He's right, Sable," continued Tinsel. "We know lots of healing magic. You're not going to die like that."

"I don't believe you!" she cried desperately. "I don't believe any of you. You're just telling us what we want to hear. You're trying to calm us with promises that nothing bad will happen because you think we're cowardly and weak."

"We don't think you're a coward," protested Tinsel mildly, but Sable wouldn't look at him anymore. "Well, we can tell you things, but you don't have to believe us. Maybe it's better if we showed you something. I've been wanting to try this." And he dropped his pack onto the snowy ground and began to rummage through it.

"Oh, good," said Seylin, looking up again. "I've been wanting to try it, too."

Sable held her breath. What were they going to try? She refused to look at the monsters; she wouldn't give them the satisfaction of seeing that she was afraid. After a minute, she felt something wet on her scarred cheek. She tried to jerk her head away, but the monster was holding her jaw.

"It's all right," he said. "It's just a cream."

Now she felt it on her other cheek. Then both cheeks grew warm, very warm, as if they were close to a fire. Alarmed, she tried to raise her hands to rub the stuff off, but he stopped her. Everyone was staring at her with intense interest. She began to panic in earnest.

"What are you doing to me?" she cried.

Tinsel turned her face, studying the cheeks with satisfaction.

"I healed your scars," he said. "I wasn't sure if it would work on such old wounds, but it did very well. There's just a thin white line left on each side."

He let go of her hands, and she reached up to touch her cheeks. They were smooth and flat now. She couldn't feel the scars at all.

"I'm glad they're not gone altogether," he added quietly. "They must have taken such courage to make."

Sable's heart was pounding. In a dream, or in a nightmare, she turned frightened eyes on the others.

"Oh, Sable, you're so beautiful!" exclaimed Irina happily.

Sable's hands began to shake. Her scars! They had kept her safe. She wasn't safe now. She didn't want those eyes staring at her anymore. She covered her cheeks with her shaking hands and turned away. The silver monster put his arms around her, shielding her from the others, and his sympathy made it harder to be brave. She moved her fingers against her cheeks, but her scars were really gone. She drew her breath in quick gasps, trying not to cry.

"You see," said Thaydar grandly to his bride, "that's the kind of magic we can do." Irina was terribly impressed. All Thorn could do was make rabbits.

"Then does that mean I won't die?" she asked in a small voice. She looked at her goblin hopefully. He always had an answer.

"My wife," growled Thaydar with conviction, "is *not* going to die in childbirth."

Irina thought about this for a minute. It wasn't hard to make up her mind.

"Then I want to be your wife," she announced, "because I don't want to die like that. When Laurel did, it really sounded like it hurt."

"You clever girl!" cried Thaydar admiringly, and that sweet face beamed up at him. Behind him, Emily grinned at Seylin and rolled her eyes.

Chapter Thirteen

They stopped a short time later to make camp in a little thicket. Tinsel took Sable off to one side and sat down, wrapping her in his cloak.

"No, I can't leave her," he said when hailed by the other busy goblins. "The last time I relied on the Leashing Spell, she tried to run off and nearly hurt herself."

Emily and Irina sat in the middle of camp while their bridegrooms set up tents. Thaydar had given Irina a necklace, and Emily watched her happily studying it in a small round mirror one of the goblin men had brought with him.

"I left my own mirror back home," she told Emily. "I wasn't awake when we left. Thaydar says when we get married I'll have a mirror so big I can see myself in it from head to toe, but I don't know how I'll be able to lift it. Do you think my present's pretty?"

"Yes," admitted Emily, noting that Thaydar had even made sure to match his fiancée's eyes. He would have been given a description of her, of course, but he wouldn't have had much time to prepare. Now, that was clever planning. No wonder he was Marak's top military man.

"Do you think I'm pretty?" continued Irina, studying her face in the glass. She looked the same as yesterday, but yesterday she had been ugly, and today she was pretty. She looked anxiously at Emily. Or maybe not?

"You're pretty," said Emily dryly. "But you're no genius."

"What's a genius?" asked Irina curiously. "Oh, wait. Thaydar'll know." Emily hadn't foreseen this development, and she didn't think Thaydar would be very pleasant about her remark.

"I just meant," she hurried to add, "that you're not terribly bright." She smiled a friendly, apologetic smile, and Irina smiled warmly back.

"Oh, I know that." She giggled. "Everybody tells me that. But I don't see what the fuss is all about."

Marak had stressed to the potential bridegrooms that they be the only ones to give their captives food. "Elf women take food from the hands of their husbands," he had warned. "If you let anyone else give their meals to them, it'll cause confusion." Irina didn't know the first thing about this, but she was only too happy to eat what Thaydar gave her. She gulped it down with relish under the loving gaze of her fiancé.

Sable understood exactly what it meant when Tinsel gave her food, and there was no way the silver goblin could induce her to eat it. Taking it would mean agreeing that he had the right to give it to her. It would mean agreeing to marriage. She wouldn't take it—she mustn't—but to turn down food freely given was a special torture for the starving woman. Her eyes wandered to it every now and then. She could even smell it a little.

"That's all right," he said kindly, laying the piece of bread in her lap. "You don't have to eat it if you don't want to, but I really think you ought to keep your strength up." And he began on his own dinner.

Keep her strength up. Of course! If Sable had the chance to escape, she would need the strength this bread would give her. Dilemma solved, she snatched the bread and began rapidly devouring it.

"Sable!" exclaimed Tinsel in alarm, plucking the bread out of her hands. "Sable, that's no way to eat!"

She stared in shattered disappointment. He'd taken the food

away from her. It was true that Thorn did this whenever she was incautious enough to let him, but she hadn't realized that this goblin would do it. Such a huge piece, too. Her eyes stung with unshed tears.

"You could make yourself really ill by bolting your food like that," observed Tinsel. "Here, eat this slowly." He tore off a bite-sized piece and handed it to her. She gazed at it dully. So tiny. The tiny piece vanished in a twinkling.

"You didn't chew that at all!" accused the goblin in dismay. "Chew this slowly," he said, holding out another piece, "and I promise I'll give you more."

Sable took the piece and gave it a couple of hasty chews to comply with his demand. He sighed and gave her more.

"Take your time," he said persuasively. "There's no need to hurry." But Sable thought there was. What if he changed his mind? She ate the next piece as rapidly as she thought he would allow, her eyes on the large amount that still remained. She had forgotten that she was supposed to refuse his food.

The party was distributed in three tents, with three people to a tent, and Sable and Tinsel were in a tent with the stripe-faced Katoo. She was glad at first that he was on the other side of her own goblin because his gruesome appearance still frightened her a little, but when Tinsel settled down beside her and spread his cloak over the two of them, Sable became very upset. Sharing food, sharing a tent, and sharing a cloak were all the signs of marriage in her simple world. She never should have taken his bread. Now this goblin thought that she was his wife. Tinsel sat up to rummage in his pack, and Sable shoved away the cloak.

"Here, let me see your hand," he said, but Sable ignored him. When she didn't respond, he pulled her hand out of the folds of her dress and rubbed cream on it. In a few seconds, the needle pricks, the knife scratches, the cooking burns, and the other scrapes and scars simply melted away. Sable stared in fascination as the skin became soft and smooth.

"How about the other hand?" he asked, and this time she held it out to him, watching as he worked in the cream. She turned her healed hands and rubbed them against each other. They had never felt like that in her memory.

Tinsel put the salve back into his pack and tucked the cloak around them once more. "Sleep well," he told her, closing his eyes, but Sable couldn't sleep. She had known the rules of her world even when she broke them, and she had known what would happen if the goblins ever came. Now they were dragging her away, but nothing was what she expected. Perhaps their confusing her like this was all just a part of the torture, but it didn't really matter. In the end, life held only two choices for her. She would either find some way to escape before she came to the goblin caves, or she would die having the monster child of her new goblin husband.

How could she escape? Now would be the best time, when they all were sleeping. If she had a knife, she could cut the side of the tent next to her and slip off into the whiteness of the day. She wasn't afraid of the daylight, she had been thrown out into it so often. One could go surprisingly far on feel alone. If they had more snow during the day, her tracks would be gone by nightfall, and they wouldn't even know which way to search.

She lay for ages listening to the goblins' steady breathing and watching the light brighten through the weave of the tent. Even under the thick canvas, the daylight made her squint. Over and over, she ran her hand along the wall of the tent beside her, pushing the seam with her fingers. If only I had a knife, she thought. If only my hand were a knife.

Suddenly the cloth parted under her fingers, and a bright beam of light stabbed in. Sable shut her eyes tightly and held her breath.

Slowly she ran her fingers along the tent wall close to the floor, and the thick, heavy cloth ripped beneath them. Very, very carefully, she made a hole that was wide enough to slip through. Then she stopped to listen. Not a sound but the goblins' breathing. Sable slid out from under the warm cloak and crawled into the daylight.

She paused outside the tent, trying to remember her surroundings. Tears streamed from her closed eyes because of the painful brightness. Crawling away between the tents, she moved as quietly as an elf knew how.

Then her hand stuck fast. It wouldn't move forward in the snow. She couldn't imagine what was wrong, and she couldn't open her eyes to see. Frantically, she slid it around, trying to find and feel the obstacle, but nothing was there to stop it. Just when she was about to give up, it freed itself as mysteriously as it had been caught, and she could move ahead once more.

Terribly excited, Sable crawled downhill, feeling for the thin trunks of the young trees. She didn't know how far the thicket extended, but she would search for a small cave or a patch of fir woods to hide in. She inched along over the uneven ground for a few minutes, and then her hand stuck fast again.

"We need to go back," said a quiet voice. It was her goblin husband.

Sable sat down and bowed her head, crushed with disappointment. "You followed me," she said.

"I had to," he answered, coming to her side. "We're leashed together with magic. You can't go more than ten feet away. The spell is like a rope that ties our hands together."

Sable rubbed her hand, remembering the pull on it. Now she understood.

"How did you cut the tent?" he asked curiously, but she wouldn't answer him. Tinsel put his arms around her, but she was stiff and unresponsive. He felt terrible for her. The poor elf woman hated him, and he couldn't do anything to make her stop.

"I'm sorry." He sighed. "I'm sorry we came and caught you. I'd let you escape, but I don't have the powder that breaks the spell. They probably knew not to give it to me. I can't steal it for you because that would be working against the King, but if there were any way I could do it, I would. I know how much you hate this. I know you want to be with your own people."

With her own people! Sable sat up with a jolt. That was what would happen if she escaped! Thorn would hunt for her, and he would find her, too. Now that the scars were gone, he would marry her, and she would die bringing his child into the world. Sable imagined for the briefest space of time what that would mean after all the insults, all the cruelty, and all the hatred that had passed between them. No torture and no goblin spells could ever be as horrible as having to be Thorn's wife.

"No!" she gasped, huddled in the goblin's arms. "I don't want my own people."

"You don't?" he echoed, surprised. He could feel that something had changed. "Sable, if you'll come with me, you won't be sorry," he promised. "I know you don't like us, but I'll be a good husband to you. Come back and get some sleep."

"All right," she answered. But there was nothing else she could say. Life held only one choice for her after all.

◠

Sable woke up screaming from one of her nightmares. She felt arms around her and heard kind words in her ear. For a few seconds, she thought that she was back with Thorn and all the intervening years had been the nightmare. That evening, she ate her husband's food without protest and responded when he spoke to her, but she didn't have much to say. She watched the monster warily, trying to see what things made him angry so that she would know what to avoid. If Thorn had taught her one thing, it was to stay out of a man's way. Life with a goblin husband would be hard enough, but it would be unbearable if he started yelling.

As they broke camp and started off, Tinsel puzzled over this new development. He found his bride's suspicious glances and careful answers even stranger than her open hostility. Yesterday she had treated him as an enemy, and he could respect and understand that. Tonight he couldn't guess what she thought he was.

"Why don't you want to go back to your own people?" he asked as they walked along.

"Because of Thorn," she said in a low voice. "He hates me, but he'll marry me anyway."

"Thorn was the rabbit-lover?" asked the silver goblin. "And you were supposed to marry him, weren't you?"

Sable nodded, unsure how much to tell him.

"When I cut my face, he didn't want to feed me anymore," she answered, "but Rowan said the band needed me. They agreed that as long as he fed me my share it didn't matter how he did it. But he hated to feed me, hated it every night. The things he did weren't so bad. It was how he looked at me."

Tinsel thought about what it would be like to live with someone who despised you.

"I couldn't do that to you," he told her. "I wouldn't ever treat you like that. And you won't die having a child, either. The goblin King can get you through it."

Sable shivered at the thought of a goblin King playing midwife.

"I'm an elf, not a goblin," she pointed out. "He doesn't know about elves."

"The goblin King's Wife is an elf," said Tinsel, "and he helped her through their son's birth. It couldn't have been too bad because she was at a banquet two days after he was born."

"Another elf?" asked Sable in surprise. "An elf I don't know? Have you seen her?"

"I see her every day," said Tinsel. "Her son's almost six now."

Sable fell silent, confused. He must be lying. Unwilling to argue with him, she listened to him make promises and explanations without comment. The young goblin kept up the one-sided conversation for a while, but then he, too, fell silent. He considered his captive bride, with her history of neglect and abuse. She was so guarded and distrustful, she would never see him as a friend.

"I can't do this," he said. "The King's going to have to find someone else to marry you."

Sable stopped and stared at him, taken aback. She thought they were already married.

"I made you angry," she guessed. "I broke a goblin rule."

"No, I'm not angry," he replied. "That's not it at all. Sable, you're beautiful and brave and smart, and I'd like the chance to make you happy. But marriage isn't going to make you happy. How can I marry you, knowing how you feel about it?"

"It's not your fault if I die," she said slowly. "It's just a woman's life."

"That's not true," said Tinsel. "If I marry you knowing it will kill you, of course it's my fault if you die, and if I marry you knowing you'll be miserable, it's my fault if you're miserable. I know you won't die, but I also know you don't believe that. I can't marry you and make you miserable."

Sable was struck by this argument. It was what she had told Thorn all those years ago. If you loved me, you wouldn't want me to die, she had said. Now, why hadn't Thorn understood that?

"But you said I'll just have to marry someone else," she pointed out unhappily.

"I know," he told her, "but that's not my decision. Marak has to decide those things; that's why he's the King."

She thought about what this would mean for her. She would still die, and she wouldn't even have this quiet goblin's kindness anymore. Maybe it would be one of those others—loud, twisted, with strange eyes. Maybe it would be somebody cruel. Maybe she would live a life like the one she had had before, only this time she would have to die anyway. Tinsel looked at her face, even more distressed now, and he guessed what she was thinking.

"Marak will let you marry anyone you choose," he said. "You're terribly important. You're almost the only elf bride we have."

Sable thought about this for some time as they walked along in silence.

"Then I'll tell him I want to marry you."

The big silver goblin was completely baffled. "Why would you do that?" he demanded.

She looked up at him anxiously.

"Will that make you angry?" she asked.

"No, it won't make me angry," insisted Tinsel, waving a hand in the air. "But you've been nothing but unhappy the whole time you've been with me. Why on earth would you want to marry me?"

No one asked Sable why she might want to do things. Even during their happiest days, Thorn hadn't been interested in hearing her point of view, and during the last several years, no one had asked her anything at all. She couldn't explain that he had understood her argument to Thorn. She couldn't really explain about his sympathy and consideration, either, that it was the first time a man had wanted to hear what she had to say.

"You're kind," she said.

"We're all kind, compared to what you're used to," he replied gloomily. "You're with a better class of people now."

"And you don't want to marry me," she continued sincerely. "I wouldn't want to marry someone who wanted to marry me."

Tinsel glanced down at her serious face, truly and deeply puzzled. "You want to marry me because I don't want to marry you," he echoed. She nodded. He fell to work on that mystery, and a thought-ful silence descended once more.

"Will he make you?" she asked after a few minutes, and he shot her an inquiring look. "Will the goblin King make you marry me?" she asked with concern.

"Oh, probably," mused Tinsel.

Sable gave a little sigh of relief.

"Then I'll tell him I won't marry anyone else."

Tinsel shook his head. "I don't see how forcing me to marry you solves any of your problems," he observed. "You're still miserable because you don't want to be married in the first place, and now I'm miserable because I don't want to be married to someone miser-able."

Sable thought about this and felt uncertain once again.

"But I'll try to be a good wife," she told him. She wasn't quite sure what that entailed. Apparently, she wasn't supposed to cook for him or sew his clothes, and she didn't know how to hunt.

"That's not really the problem," explained Tinsel. "You'd still think I was trying to kill you, and you couldn't help hating me for it. Remember that look in the elf man's eyes that you didn't want to see?" She nodded. "Well, I don't want to see it, either."

A light dawned in Sable's mind. She had been afraid that he would get angry and hate her, and it turned out that he was afraid she would hate *him*. She didn't just need his kindness, he needed her kindness, too. Sable was staggered at the thought. She had never had

that kind of power before. Thorn had never given her the least indication that he cared about what she thought of him.

"But what if you don't see it?" she asked him. "If I don't get
angry at you? If I try to be kind, too?"

Tinsel stopped walking. He studied her for a long minute.

"If that's what you want, Sable," he said, and he smiled.

Sable didn't know what to do. Maybe it was all a trick. Maybe,
when they got to the caves, this goblin would hand her over to be tortured. But he didn't look as if he would, and he had been a good
husband so far. He had fed her and kept her warm and talked to her,
and he had cared about how she felt.

She rubbed her healed hands together, thinking about this. Then
she looked up and managed a smile in return.

"We'll have a happy year," she whispered. "I promise."

Chapter Fourteen

Camp that morning was surprisingly uneventful. They had made good time during the long winter night and would be home before midnight the next day. Richard cheerfully ran errands for anyone who asked, and the goblin men made a fuss over him. He had assisted in unloading Dinner, who had been a packhorse for the night, and now he was bringing a pot of water to Brindle.

"Light that fire for me," directed the man, and a roaring flame shot up. "Wait! Not so much force next time!"

Richard sat down by the fire to tend it, and Brindle began sorting through their supplies.

"You have a good bit of magic," he observed to Richard. "If you're Mandrake's boy, and Marak thinks you are, you come by it naturally. Mandrake was the best illusionist among the Guard in his day. You'd walk right by him and think he was a rock or a tree. Then he'd trip you and get a good laugh at the stupid look on your face."

"I have a dad?" asked Richard in amazement.

"Doesn't everybody?" noted Brindle. "Had a dad, is more like it. Mandrake died a couple of years ago, and that's lucky for him. Marak was so angry when he found out about you that I thought he'd kill us all. I'm not even old enough to be your dad, and I still shook in my boots."

Richard's face fell. "The King didn't like it, eh?"

"Didn't like it?! He set a door on fire just by touching it, he was in such a temper! He called in every man who had been outside the

171

kingdom, and he said that if anything like that ever happened again we'd every one of us be sorry."

"I've never been the kind who could please a king," said the boy with a sigh.

"Don't worry," said Brindle. "It's not your problem. Look here, now. Watch me make these beans jump into the pot."

"Lumme!" exclaimed Richard, and Brindle laughed at his expression.

"It's better with bacon, but we didn't bring any. Here, I'll teach you the spell."

Sable fell asleep fairly easily, but she woke up screaming again. She was very apprehensive about leaving the world she knew and going down into the goblin caves. As the evening wore on and they drew closer to the kingdom, she became quieter and quieter.

"Are you sure the goblin King will let me marry you, Tinsel?" she asked anxiously.

"I'm positive," said Tinsel. "He wants you to be happy."

"I don't know why he would want that," said Sable suspiciously. "Not if he's the goblin King."

The goblin King figured very prominently in the elves' scary stories. Human slaves had modified many of these from the ghost stories they knew in order to entertain the little elf children. The goblin King acted in some like a ghost, in some like an ogre, and in some like the devil himself. What he almost never acted like was an authentic goblin King, but Sable didn't know that.

Tinsel knew perfectly well why the goblin King would want her to be happy. Marak had reminded the whole party about it before they had left. The First Fathers of the two races were tremendously intelligent, but they were something like amateur experimenters. Neither elves nor goblins reproduced with the careless ease of the human race. Elf women didn't have the problem of sterility that goblins often had, but they were terribly sensitive to their surroundings. Unhappy elf women bore only one child, whereas happy ones bore three or four. Marak needed as many children as he could get from these last remaining elves to shore up his magical high families, and he had made very sure that his goblins understood this.

The party had been skirting forested hills for some time, and Sable could tell by their excited chatter that the goblins were nearing home. Now they left the forest to cross rolling fields again, and she felt a little relieved. There couldn't be a cave out here, she thought. But she was wrong.

"Close your eyes," warned Tinsel. "I don't want you to be frightened." Faint with dread, she felt them walking down a long slope.

When Tinsel uncovered her eyes, Sable gasped. They weren't in a field anymore. They were walking through a long, thin cavern, and her sky was now black stone. The light was very bright, and she could see that not one thing lived here, not a plant, not a field mouse, not a bug. They came to the end of this cavern, and a metal wall faced them. They were trapped, thought Sable in a panic. They would die here in this dead place.

"Welcome, elf brides!" boomed a massive voice, and Sable cringed in fear. "It's so nice to see pretty elves again." The iron wall swung forward, and the party walked through. Then it shut with a clang. "Do come see me sometimes," it invited, "even though I can't let you out."

The next cave was large, and horses lived in it; Sable could see their long faces poking out from little rooms on the sides. But the ceiling of this huge room seemed so low, she felt as if it were pushing down to crush her. She felt sick, and she found that she was shaking from head to foot.

From the stable they entered a suite of rooms designed for the reception and marriage of elves, where the goblin men removed the

Leashing Spell at a large basin of water. They stopped in a big square waiting room decorated with lavish magnificence, the walls and ceiling covered with golden mosaics of the design that the dwarves liked best. To please the other races, dwarves sometimes made stone plants and flowers, but they never understood the point of making a rock look like something it wasn't. Their own art aimed at bringing out the natural beauty of stone and metal in intricate progressions and patterns of different colors.

Sable blinked in the bright light and studied the ceiling right above her, dazzled by the glittering tiles. She longed for the simple clutter of the forest, with its living creatures, its gentle movements, and its high, high ceiling of stars.

When she looked down again, a new goblin was standing before them. He was hideous, with eyes of two colors and stiff hair that rustled and moved like a living thing. His lips were brown, as if they were smeared with dried blood; his teeth were like sharp metal knives; and his skin was dreadfully pale, as if he were one of the walking dead.

"Welcome, elf brides, to my kingdom," the corpselike wraith said pleasantly. "And while I understand that you aren't yet glad to be here, you may rest assured that I am very glad to have you here. An especially warm welcome to Sable," and those eyes slid to her face. "It's been many a long year since we greeted a lord's daughter in this room." The bicolor eyes, brilliant in that deathly paleness, bored into her like coals. Sable shivered and hid her face against Tinsel's chest.

"During the journey," continued the voice, "you have had some time to become acquainted with the bridegrooms I picked out for you. I don't expect you to be pleased about your marriages, but if you have any specific objections to make about your bridegrooms, I will be happy to listen to them and see what I can do. Irina, please come with me. Thaydar will wait for you. We'll talk for a few minutes in the next room, and then you'll come back here."

Marak walked into a small room that was decorated as lavishly as the larger one. Against the far wall stood an elaborate stone throne that was carved out of one block. Before the throne was a stone table, its gray-veined surface highly polished, and on the other side of the table was a simple square stool of stone protruding from the floor.

Marak crossed to the throne and sat down on it, considering the elf girl before him. Less sensitive than Sable, Irina was also better prepared. She had been listening to Thaydar's stories about the goblin King for the last two nights, and she even knew something about what he would look like. Nevertheless, she was taken aback by his bizarre appearance and by all the unfamiliar sights. She wished Thaydar could be there with her.

"Please sit down," Marak urged, gesturing to the stool beside her. Irina looked at the stone seat without much comprehension. Elves didn't use furniture, so she wasn't accustomed to chairs. When she continued to stand, Marak left the matter alone.

"Tell me, do you have any objection to marrying Thaydar?" he asked. "Has anything he's said or done upset you?"

Irina's eyes were wandering in a bewildered manner around the room and back to him. She had thought she understood what her new life would be like, but now she was beginning to doubt it. Maybe Sable was right. Maybe Thaydar had just been telling her what she wanted to hear.

"He said—he said—that I wouldn't have to butcher," she stammered, looking at the King a little anxiously.

"That upset you?" asked Marak, amused. But he didn't laugh. Kate had specifically warned him not to.

"Oh! No," amended Irina. "I really hate to butcher."

"I promise you won't have to," said the goblin King graciously, and the girl relaxed a little.

"Do you like Thaydar?" he asked with interest.

"Oh, yes," confided Irina. "He knows all kinds of things, and he's just so strong and scary, and he doesn't ever let anybody tease me."

"Did my goblins tease you?" asked Marak in surprise.

"No," said Irina, "but he would have pummeled them if they had. And he said I could have, oh, all kind of things, dresses and mirrors and presents." She looked at the goblin King hopefully. She was starting to regain her confidence.

"He'll give them to you," promised Marak. "Thaydar is a very important goblin in this kingdom, and he can have anything he wants. You're right that he knows things. He's my military commander, and he advises me. If I were to die, he would take over running the kingdom until my son was old enough to rule."

"Oh," said Irina, tremendously impressed. Kings and kingdoms sounded so grand. "Thaydar says I'm pretty," she told him with innocent satisfaction. "He says I'm the prettiest thing he ever saw."

"I'm sure he wouldn't lie," commented the goblin King helpfully.

"Am I the prettiest thing you ever saw?" she asked. Marak fixed her with a thoughtful gaze.

"No," he answered steadily. "My wife is the prettiest thing I ever saw."

Irina considered this.

"I think that's so sweet," she said, beaming at him. Marak propped his chin on his hands and gave her an encouraging smile.

"So you don't mind marrying Thaydar," he concluded. "Is there anything else that's worrying you? Anything you'd like to mention?"

"There is one thing," she confessed reluctantly. "I'm not old enough to be married yet, not for six months."

"So you're seventeen?" inquired the goblin King.

"I don't know," said Irina.

"I think it would be fine for you to be married now," said Marak cautiously, watching her face. "Does that bother you?"

"No," answered the elf girl carelessly. "Thaydar says it's just a lot of nonsense."

Marak grinned. "I'm sure he's right," he said. "Thaydar knows all kinds of things."

⌒

The group waited quietly in the large room. Long stone benches ringed the walls on three sides, but no one sat down.

The door opened, and Irina emerged.

"Sparks came out of my hand," she giggled to her bridegroom.

"That's wonderful!" said Thaydar warmly.

Seylin smiled to himself. It wasn't exactly wonderful. Marak had tested her for magical ability, and she was moderately but not thrillingly gifted. Emily sighed. When he had tested her, not even one spark had shown up.

"Sable," called Marak from the door. He could tell that the other elf was almost fainting with fear. Excellent, he thought with well-concealed glee. Her magical instinct was alert to the danger of goblins, the same sixth sense that had kept Kate fighting to stay away from him. Sable was an aristocrat, there was no doubt about it.

It's a trick, thought Sable, beside herself with dread. She would go through the door, and they would lock her up; they would torture her and work horrible magic. When Tinsel let her go, she clung to his hands.

"It's all right," he told her in a low voice. "I'll be waiting right here."

She remembered her dignity. She walked quietly into the small room, her eyes on the floor, somehow managing to pass the goblin King. She didn't look around as Irina had because she didn't want to see what was coming. When she heard the door shut behind her, she closed her eyes tightly. Marak walked by her and around the table, studying her attentively as he passed.

"Sable, please sit down," he invited. "And you'll need to open your eyes in order to find your seat," he added helpfully.

Sable stole a quick glance around the room, found the stone stool, and sat down on its edge, head down, clutching her hands together tightly.

"The direct descendant of the noble family Sabul," mused Marak, looking at his prize capture with acquisitive eyes. "One of the elf King's eighteen camp lords, among the highest of the high elves. There is nothing in a goblin King's power that I wouldn't do to make you happy in your marriage and happy in my kingdom. And look at me when I speak to you," he added pleasantly. "That's how business is conducted."

Sable glanced up at him, wincing. Marak smiled at her.

"That's better," he said. "I don't look as bad as you think. I want you to be happy, Sable. I want it very badly. So why don't you tell me what's bothering you because you don't look very happy at the moment."

"I can't live down here!" she burst out desperately. "Nothing lives here, not a tree, not a blade of grass. I can't even remember how many doors are between me and the stars now, and I can't breathe anymore!"

"Spoken like a true elf," remarked the goblin King approvingly. "We'll take those problems one at a time. The feeling of not being able to breathe is called claustrophobia, and it's very common in new elf brides. The thing to remember is that air can pass freely through spaces where you are not permitted to go. Even in small rooms like this one, you can usually feel moving air. Do this." He held his hand up in front of him, and Sable raised her shaking hand to copy. She could feel a tiny breeze flowing past it, and her breathing relaxed slightly.

"Blades of grass. We have lots and lots of those, and we have lots of sheep that eat them. We don't allow either one indoors, but you can visit them anytime you like. Trees. We don't have any real trees, but we do have a grove of pretend trees put in for the sake of the elves. They won't fool you, but you may find they do you a certain amount of good anyway, and if you decide you don't like them, please do me a favor and don't breathe a word of it to the dwarves.

"Stars," he continued. "Stars we don't have, no stars of any kind. Elf brides in the old days simply had to live without them, and they weren't happy about that. But you don't have a race of kinsmen outside waiting to liberate you, so I think I can offer you a compro⁄ mise. As long as I see you trying to settle into kingdom life, I'll let you go outside for the night of each full moon. Do you think that will help make up for the lack of stars?"

Sable had been afraid she would never see the night sky again, but now she would see it in just three weeks. She began to lose her fright of the wraithlike goblin King, and the relief showed on her face. Tinsel was telling the truth, and so was he. He did want her to be happy.

"My goblins have relayed to me your fears about childbirth and the shocking condition of life in your camp," continued Marak. "I want to assure you that what was normal in your camp is not normal at all, and I certainly wouldn't authorize your marriage if I thought death would be the result."

"Why would you care?" she whispered. "It's just what happens."

"I care because you're my prisoner and not my subject," he responded. "I could order one of my subjects to certain death, in battle, for instance, if that death were truly necessary. But you're a defenseless prisoner who has committed no crime, so I can't have you killed no matter what the profit might be. It would be demeaning to my kingship."

There was a small silence, and Sable decided that he expected her to speak.

"Thank you for explaining that you don't think I'll die," she said.

"But you don't believe me," commented the goblin King. He paused and thought for a minute.

"Beauty meant everything to the First Fathers of the elves," he reflected. "It's a goal that causes problems in elf magic and elf culture, but nowhere is the problem of beauty so great as when the elf woman goes into labor. You elf women are petite and slender, with lovely, tiny bones, but an elf baby is longer-limbed and older than babies of other races, not like an ugly newborn at all. When a fine-boned, small elf woman tries to deliver this larger, older baby, death is the logical result. With magic, birth is uncomfortable but achievable. Without magic, another process eventually sets in which usually allows the child to be born but always takes the life of the mother."

Sable found it hard to believe that magic could make such a difference and that all the elf men in her band would lie. "We were told that women have to die so babies can be born," she said. "Magic might just help sometimes."

"So you would say that the occasional woman might be saved by magic," suggested Marak, "but that the race was set up with the mother's death in mind." Sable nodded. "Not possible, and I can prove it to you." He hesitated. "At least, I think I can," he added, looking at her sharply. "Have you learned any math at all? Anything about numbers?"

"Do you mean counting?" asked Sable. "I can count up to eighteen."

"It's like counting," Marak said, "and you're smart, even if you're untaught. We'll give it a try. The race of elves came from fifteen First Fathers, and at one point in history there were about four thousand elves. That's a huge number, Sable—that's like counting the stars in the sky."

Sable was impressed. So many elves. So much company. How nice it would have been.

"Now, you notice that the number gets bigger, much bigger. Let's see if we can do that when the mother dies in childbirth."

He pulled open a shallow drawer in the table and brought out some shiny gold objects that looked like sharp pins sticking up from flat bases. Sable watched him, secretly a little flattered. Only her father had ever tried to teach her things. Thorn didn't usually explain himself at all. He just insisted that he was right.

"Here is your elf couple," said the goblin King, setting up two of the golden spikes before her. "A man and his wife. But the woman can have only one child, and then she dies."

He advanced another pin. "Here's the child. It took two parents to produce only one child. When the older generation dies away," and he covered up the two pins with his hand, "there won't be more elves than before. The mother has left a child to replace herself, but the father has no child to replace him."

Sable stared at the pins. She thought about Alder and Rose having just Irina, and Hemlock and May having just Willow. There weren't more elves than before, there were fewer.

"But the man could marry another wife," she pointed out. That was what Father had done to replace himself.

"Very good," said Marak approvingly. "Yes, that will help, but will it help enough?"

He brought out two more pins. "Here's the new wife, and she has a child. Now we have two children, that's true, but look, it took three parents to make them. You can see that you won't ever have more elves later if the mother dies. You'll always have fewer and fewer. But we know that the elves went the other way, that there were more and more. That happened because elf women were having two, three, and four children apiece, and that means elf women aren't supposed to die in childbirth."

Sable stared at the pins in excitement. It all made perfect sense. She knew that there had been more elves in her father's day. Even she had seen the band shrink in her lifetime. Soon, none of them would be left. Surviving childbirth. Who would have imagined that a goblin would teach her that?

Marak watched her excited face, pleased with his quick pupil. "Aside from this, did you have any other concerns?" he asked. "Do you have any objection to marrying Tinsel?"

"I won't marry anyone else," declared Sable forcefully. "He's kind."

"He is, indeed—very kind," agreed the goblin King. "Tinsel's always been amazingly nice. Since you have no objection, we'll hold the marriage shortly, and now I'd like to test you for magical ability."

He stood up and walked around the table toward her. Sable jumped up and drew back in alarm.

"Magical ability?" she asked. "What do you mean?"

"Your ability to work magic, of course," he said, amused. "What else would I mean?"

"But women can't work magic," she protested, taking another step back, and the goblin King gave a chuckle.

"I'm afraid your upbringing has been absolutely appalling," he said cheerfully. "No one has bothered to teach you anything but lies. Not only can elf women work magic, but certain kinds of elf magic were always worked by the women. Hold out your hand, and I'll show you."

Sable held out her hand, looking away and shuddering with disgust as he put that corpse's hand over hers. He pointed absently at the lamp above him, and the room darkened. Her hand began glowing with a bright silver light, and a single ray like a moonbeam shot from the end of each finger. The beams played around the shadowy room as she moved her fingers, and the silver light didn't fade for almost a minute.

"I knew it," gloated the goblin King, pointing at the lamp again. "You're powerfully magical, probably as magical as Seylin is. I'll start teaching you magic myself right away. You and Irina can learn with my wife; she's a beginner, too. Most magical people have a special talent. My wife's is killing people. I wouldn't be surprised, Sable, if yours is healing, and that's why you were so upset by the childbirth deaths. It would be wonderful if you were a healer; a talented elf healer could do a lot of good in my kingdom."

Sable flexed her hand, staring at it, and thought of Thorn and Rowan and Willow laughing over her working magic. And all the time, she could do it. She just needed to be taught. The goblin King opened the door, and she walked out, but she wasn't the same woman who had walked in a short time before. Her head was high, and her eyes were shining. She wasn't going to be tortured, and she wasn't going to die. She was going to learn magic.

"Your turn, M," announced Marak.

The second she was inside the door, Emily threw herself into his arms. "I've missed you so much!" she cried.

"Well!" exclaimed Marak, hugging her in return. "I'd like you to remember that this is an official elf bride's interview. You'll want to save these disruptive demonstrations for a more appropriate moment, such as the next time I'm trying to hold court."

Emily released him. "I count as an elf bride?" she demanded.

"Seylin went out hunting for a bride, and it seems to me that he's found one."

"I went out hunting for Seylin," countered Emily with a grin, "and I'm the one who found what I was after."

"You were seeking your human nature," corrected the goblin King, smiling. "Tell me, how did that go?"

Emily sobered up, thinking about what she'd found on her quest, about the elf girl's book and her goblin son's disastrous war of revenge.

"I found out that you don't just grow up into the person you should become," she said. "I always thought that it happened on its own, but it actually takes a lot of work. And sometimes"—she thought about Whiteye standing on the battlefield reading his mother's book—"sometimes it doesn't happen at all."

Marak watched her pensive face, a little surprised.

"That's certainly true," he remarked. "What else did you find out?"

"I found out that if you learn enough about something you can't hate it even if you want to. That's why Ruby couldn't hate the human twins." She paused to consider that and gave a little sigh. "And I suppose that's why I couldn't hate Ruby, either. What did you decide, Marak? You're letting her keep the children, aren't you?"

"Yes, I am, until they grow up," replied the goblin King. "Then Jack will have to leave. I'm not letting him bring a wife down here and start populating my kingdom with humans. I'll have him taught the merchant's craft, and he can make trading trips with the men. That's something that should help him in his world. Ruby is settling down with them on a farm across the valley. I should have known that if I sent her out with you she'd never do any more teaching."

"Ha! I was good for her," retorted Emily. "I made her think about new things."

"That I believe," said Marak. "You never think the same old things that the rest of us do. I've missed you, too—very much. No one else causes me such interesting problems. And let me add that seeing you and Seylin married will fulfill my fondest hopes for you both."

Emily stared at him in astonishment.

"Marak!" she exclaimed. "I never knew that."

"I know," he observed. "You never asked me. I've lived more than three times as long as you have, you know. You might ask my advice on occasion."

Marak opened the door and called in the rest of the group. Then he sat down on the throne again and lifted a large book onto the table. He flipped through the book until he came to the first blank page, produced a bottle of ink, and selected a quill pen from the drawer.

"The registry and marriage of elf brides," he informed the small crowd before him, "is a simple ceremony with three distinct parts. I'm going to perform each part for all three of you before moving on to the next one. M, you're first."

He beckoned Emily and Seylin up to the table. Then he positioned one of Sable's golden pins before them and set a small golden disk beside it. "Prick her finger," he directed Seylin, "and squeeze two drops of blood onto this disk."

Emily was preparing to question whether this was really necessary, but Seylin had her finger pricked before she could protest. The King covered the small disk with his six-fingered hand. When he removed it, the disk had changed color. It was now almost entirely bright red, but one small sliver appeared to have been marked off with a straight line, and beyond that line it was white.

"There, M, is your human blood," explained Marak, pointing to the red part with his quill. "And there's the elf blood," he went on, pointing to the slim white section. Emily studied it unhappily. No wonder her magic spells never worked.

Marak picked up his quill and dipped it, entering her into the registry. "Your age?" he asked.

"Eighteen," answered Emily. He entered it along with the results of the test and then added Seylin's name and age below it.

"Humor me, Seylin," said Marak as he wrote. "I want to test you, too."

Seylin obediently pricked his own finger and squeezed blood onto a new disk. When Marak lifted his hand from it, Seylin's disk showed three colors. Almost the entire disk was white, but a small section was red, and the tiniest of slivers was black.

"You see," said the King, "you're not an elf at all. Here's your elvish blood." He pointed to the white section. "That's quite a bit, but elves aren't like goblins. They never marry other races if they have any choice at all, and only the women can. An elf man couldn't have children with an elf cross, not even one as powerful as Kate. No elf would ever call you an elf. Do you see this?" he added, pointing to the tiny black section. "That's your goblin blood, so you're a goblin. One drop is all it takes."

Irina's disk was totally white.

"Now, that's an elf," observed Marak with satisfaction. "Is she seventeen, Sable?" And when Sable nodded, he entered her age. Then he wrote Thaydar's information below hers.

"Sable," continued Marak. "Sabul," he added, writing the characters. "'Igniting the red flames.'" He paused and put down his quill to study the black-haired elf woman before him.

"In the reign of Aganir Halbi, the elf King named Winter Frost," he said, "and in the reign of my ancestor Marak the Antlered, the goblin King's military commander claimed the honor of an elf bride, and he and his men attacked the Top Shield Star Camp. The camp lord fell in that battle, and so did his son, but a young elf turned the tide. He fought so fiercely that he killed the goblin commander himself, along with a number of the Guard, and no elf brides were taken that night. As a reward, the elf King gave that young man the lordship of the camp along with a new name, Sabul, the Raging Fire because he had fought like a raging fire among the goblins."

Sable stared at the goblin King in astonishment. "How do you know that?" she asked.

"I read it in the chronicles," replied Marak. "Both of them. We have the elvish chronicles, too, for that span of years."

Sable didn't even feel the prick. A raging fire. Sabul. She remembered her father with a surge of compassion. He'd been hard on them, but he'd been hard on himself, too, and she wished she could find his spirit somewhere and tell him about the first Lord Sabul.

"Pure elf," commented Marak, glancing at the white disk. "How old are you, Sable?" She came out of her daydream with a jolt.

"I don't know the number for it," she confessed, ashamed.

"Tell me what you know about it," suggested Marak. "We can probably find the number."

"Irina and I share the same birthday moon," began Sable slowly, thinking about numbers. "We were both born in the middle month at the summer camp. When I reached my marriage moon, that meant I was eighteen, but at that same moon, Irina was only twelve. She won't be eighteen until that moon comes back next summer."

"Very good," said the goblin King. "You were eighteen five years ago, so that means you're twenty-three now. Next summer, you'll be twenty-four." He wrote down her age and Tinsel's information below it. Sable stared at him in awe and thought about all the things he knew: elvish and reading and writing and magic and enough numbers to count the stars in the sky. She wondered what it would be like to know so much, and how long it must have taken to learn.

"That completes the registry," said Marak, blotting the page and setting the book aside. "Now I need to put a magical symbol on you so that the doors know not to let you out." He took a bottle of gold ink and a small paintbrush from the drawer and worked the magic on Irina. "And remember, Sable, that I'll let you out for the full moon. Don't try to fight the spell." He worked the magic and studied the letter, but Sable didn't show the burning that Kate had after her own wedding ceremony.

"Very good," said Marak, putting down the ink and brush. "Now we come to the Binding Spell, which is the actual marriage. Seylin and M, you're first," he added, coming over to them. He plucked a hair from Emily's head and wrapped it around Seylin's right wrist. Then he plucked a hair from Seylin's head and wrapped it around Emily's wrist. As he wrapped the hair, it seemed to vanish from his fingers, but the hair could still be seen, deep under the skin, encircling the wrist like a thread. Irina came closer to look, and Emily held out her wrist so that she could see.

"This magic," explained Marak, "ensures that the goblin genealogies are accurate. As long as the married couple remain true to each other, those hairs can't be felt. If a spouse commits adultery, the hair begins to itch, and a rash spreads up and down the arm. That itch only stops when the spouse names the other guilty party in front of the King, so I can correct the genealogies if necessary, and in front of the other spouse, so he or she can decide on a suitable revenge. But the worst revenge is that the entire kingdom knows about it," he concluded cheerfully. "The confessions always take place at court, and they're very well attended."

The goblin King turned to his new couple.

"Congratulations on your marriage," he said pleasantly, "and because you certainly won't want to take her back to your Guard quarters, Seylin, the goblins have decorated M's quarters instead. That required doing some cleaning, M, so if you can't find anything, ask Kate where she had things put. Seylin, come see me tomorrow about new employment that will change your living quarters."

The young pair received the congratulations of the others and left the room, going back through the stables and down the corridor that had been Emily's first view of the goblin kingdom. They paused to lean out a window together, as they had done on that first night. The view of the lake valley, crossed by twinkling lights, seemed one of the most beautiful sights in the world.

Marak performed the Binding Spell on Thaydar and Irina, and now Irina had a hair of her own to study, black against the whiteness of her slender wrist.

"Congratulations on your marriage, old friend," said the King, "and, Irina, I hope you'll be very happy. Kate left some clothes in the dressing room for you to try on until you can have your own clothes made."

Thaydar and Irina left the room together, leaving Sable rather stunned.

"But—she isn't married now, surely?" she asked in confusion. "Irina's still just a child."

"It's all right, Sable," said Marak reassuringly. "I know that rule about waiting until the marriage moon is very important in elvish society, but it's never been true among the goblins. Of course, if Irina were younger, she wouldn't be ready for marriage, but she's seventeen, and that's old enough."

As Sable mulled this over, the goblin King performed the Binding Spell, and she was soon captivated by the sight of a thick silver thread shining around her wrist. She raised her arm and turned it, watching the silver sparkle in the bright light, and Tinsel smiled at the serious look on her face.

"Congratulations to both of you," said Marak. "Tinsel, spend the week with your wife, and keep her away from crowds. You've been moved into the most elaborate of the elf-bride quarters, on the green level. You'll find that your role as husband to an elf lord's daughter is more important to the kingdom than your role as a member of the King's Guard, and I know you'll treat it as such. I hope you'll both be very happy. In fact, I insist on it."

The goblin King watched the sober young pair leave the room hand in hand. As they went through the large square room, he saw Sable glance apprehensively at the ceiling, and he made a mental note to check up on her claustrophobia after a couple of days. Then he turned and surveyed all the clutter the ceremonies had created. Tomorrow, he would come back and retrieve the elf brides' registry and the magical items. He still had one more important errand to perform before he could sleep tonight.

Richard had managed to elude all adult supervision. Emily had left the stable convinced that he was with Brindle, and Brindle was sure he had seen the boy with Emily. It was hardly surprising that Richard could accomplish this. Even without an expert illusionist for a father, he had lived long enough on the streets to know how to make himself disappear.

Once Richard's companions left, goblin servants emerged to take care of Dinner. They examined the new horse carefully, gave him a thorough grooming, and prepared him a hot mash to eat. While he enjoyed his meal, they argued over his various features and faults. Finally, they turned him loose in a princely stall of his own, cleaned up the area, and left. Richard watched everything from behind some grain sacks, taking care not to attract attention.

As soon as the stables were quiet, he hurried back to the iron door and felt all over its smooth surface for a latch.

"What are you doing?" inquired a booming voice. "Didn't I just let you in?"

The boy looked around the empty corridor, but no one was there.

"Which one of you said that?" he demanded bravely.

"Which one of us?" The voice was puzzled. "I just see you and me. And stop that!" it continued as he slid his fingers over the hinges. "I'm very ticklish!"

Richard's mouth formed an O.

"I don't believe it!" he breathed. "It's the blinking door, isn't it? Well, if you're the door, then you can just let me out!"

"Sorry," replied the door officiously. "No minors allowed outside without their parents."

"But I'm not one of your miners!" exclaimed the boy. "I've never been in a mine before now!"

"You're confusing me," remarked the door. "I never open when I'm confused."

Richard began pounding on the iron surface.

"I'm built to withstand that," it observed stoically.

"Listen, if you don't open up right now, I'll—"

"Good evening, goblin King."

Richard froze, his heart in his mouth. The authorities had him at last.

"Good evening, door," replied a pleasant voice. "Good evening, Richard. Why are you beating up my door? Are you going so soon?"

The terrified boy huddled against the iron surface, his eyes tightly shut.

"Your Majesty, if you'll just let me out," he whispered, "you'll never see me again."

"I've no doubt of that," remarked the voice. "Why would I want to let you out?"

"You don't want me here," insisted Richard desperately. "You've been angry about me from the start. I know what you think. You think I'm not good enough to be one of your goblins. You think I'm trash," he concluded miserably. "And you'd be right about that."

"I think you're very smart, and I'm impressed at your character. Now, why don't you turn around and look at me?"

The street urchin shook his head and kept his eyes shut.

"No, you're talking like a real gentleman," he said dolefully, "but it's best if I just go. I'll go back to the life I'm used to. I'd rather."

"You'd rather?" The voice was closer. "You'd rather not have a home or a King?"

"No." The boy gave a sigh. "I'd rather not even think about them."

"That's unfortunate because you have them anyway." A firm hand pulled him around, and he looked into two piercing eyes.

Richard burst into tears.

"I'm sorry!" he wailed. "For everything! Don't send me away! I couldn't bear it, I tell you. You'd kill me! Please don't send me away!" He wrapped his skinny arms around his King and wept noisily on his shirtfront.

"That's better," commented Marak, patting the sobbing boy on the head. "So you were running away before I could send you away."

"It's the worst thing I know," explained the boy tearfully. "I couldn't bear it happening again."

"No, you couldn't," agreed his monarch. "I'm surprised you survived it before. Being alone is the worst thing that can happen to a goblin, and it shouldn't ever have a chance to happen. That's why I was so angry when I heard about you all alone out there. I certainly wasn't angry at you."

Richard considered this through his tears.

"I don't know what you're going to do with me, Your Majesty," he said sadly. "All I know is picking pockets and scaring people in a show. I can't do anything but steal and lift handkerchiefs and wallets. Except—I do know how to make beans jump into a pot."

Marak laughed. "You have one honest pursuit, anyway! With a

talent like that, you'll never go hungry. Come along. Tomorrow, I'll take you to the pages' floor, and you can meet the other children, but tonight you can stay with my family."

The urchin wiped his streaming eyes with the back of his hand.

"Bless me!" he exclaimed in wonder. "Me stay with a king and queen and all, just like I was somebody!"

"And a prince, too," pointed out Marak. "I don't mind if you teach my son how to pick pockets, but keep that bean trick to your-self. He would love it, and Kate's very particular about his manners. Let's go wake her up now, Richard. She's been anxious to meet you." And the King of the ugly people led his new subject away in search of a place to belong.

Chapter Fifteen

Sable and Tinsel went through the endless halls and stairwells of the palace, and one long, thin, bright cave replaced another before the apprehensive woman's field of view. Somehow, she was supposed to find a way to live in this strange series of boxes upon boxes.

But when they opened the door of their new living quarters, Sable didn't see a sterile box. The large, open room had been designed to look as much like a stretch of forest as possible. A number of artificial trees stood here and there, and green mats and hangings simulated the ferns and vines of a woodland scene. Over it all stretched a dull black ceiling so high that it failed to attract notice. An ornamental pool sparkled by the door under the shadow of some green-hung saplings. A little fountain bubbled at one end of it, and small silver fish flashed through the water beneath polished stone water-lilies.

The elf woman found that she was able to breathe freely for the first time since coming underground. It wasn't that the pretend trees fooled her. They just made the place look right to her. In the same way that Tinsel would have recognized a chair whether it was wood, stone, or metal, Sable recognized the organic clutter and jumble that belonged to a proper forest camp. And when they climbed the steps notched into the short cliff face that led up to their sleeping area, there stood a tent. The goblin studied it with a puzzled smile, wondering at a tent indoors, but Sable crawled into it to test the thickness of the pallet and crawled back out again, her face shining. She had never slept anywhere except inside a tent. Sleeping in a bed would have made her feel very unsafe.

They went back downstairs to the ornamental pool and discovered that supper had been left there in a basket. Tinsel opened a bottle of beer while Sable contemplated the enormous bun that he had handed her. Mindful of his gaze, she tried to eat it slowly, but the food only worried and upset her. For years, she had existed from one meal to the next. Life was a fragile, precarious thing.

"Maybe I'll be happy here," she said, not looking at her new husband. She rose and began to walk about, pausing to run her hand over the cloth greenery.

"Of course you will," agreed Tinsel in an encouraging tone. "You know the goblin King wants you to."

"But should I be happy?" demanded Sable. "My father taught me to hate goblins. Now I'm doing what they want." She thought about the goblin King, with his brilliance and learning. Her enemy seemed to know everything. Maybe he even knew at this moment that she was considering defying him. "What do you think he would do to me, Tinsel, if I'm not happy here?"

"Marak? I don't know. He has books to help him with that kind of thing, but I'm sure he wouldn't hurt you."

Sable imagined the goblin King poring over his books, looking up the perfect remedy for a rebellious elf. She shuddered. It wouldn't matter whether he hurt her or not; she knew she didn't have the courage to stand against him. She thought about her father, strong and brave, and felt again the pain of breaking faith with him. She knelt by the little pool to watch the silver fish.

"My father said that the goblins took the cowards. That's why I'm here," she whispered.

"That's not true." Her goblin came to put an arm around her.

"You were right not to marry. Your father was wrong about a woman's life. No woman should feel it's her duty to die having a child."

"I was right about that, wasn't I?" Sable studied her reflection. "The men lied to us for years and years. My father told me elf women were supposed to die. He probably lied to me about goblins, too."

"I'm sure he did," said Tinsel. "You don't have to hate us." But Sable didn't respond. She knew her father hadn't really lied about goblins. He just hadn't known how clever they were. He would never have given in like this and done what the goblin King wanted. She felt discouraged and overwhelmed.

"I don't care if he lied or not!" she cried bitterly. "I don't care what he taught me to do. I want to be happy. I want to learn magic, and I want to learn about numbers. Tinsel, would you teach me?"

The silver goblin hugged her reassuringly. "If that's what makes you happy," he promised.

Sable looked at him with new understanding. "I heard the goblin King tell you that I'm more important than your other work. You're just like me. If we're not happy, he'll look up remedies for you, too."

"I suppose so." Tinsel gave a rueful smile. "They might not be pleasant, either. He wouldn't worry so much about hurting me."

Sable smiled back, feeling a surge of sympathy and gratitude. It felt good to share her captivity with a fellow pawn.

"Then we'll have to look after each other," she concluded, "and make sure he doesn't need his books. I'm thirsty, Tinsel. Is cave water safe to drink?"

Next morning, Seylin went to see the goblin King to discuss his new employment, but he had a question to ask first.

"Why did it fulfill your fondest hopes when Em and I married?" he wanted to know. Marak gave him a sidelong glance.

"It isn't enough that you two have always loved each other and that I myself am very fond of you both?"

The young man considered this for a minute. Then he shook his head. "Not to make it a fondest hope," he declared.

"Then perhaps I should add," remarked the goblin King cheerfully, "that, with your overpowering elf blood and M's overpowering human blood, you'll have far more children than in a normal goblin marriage. My hope is that your children will have practically no goblin blood in them, and I'd say there will be seven or eight at least."

"You want me to have eight children?" demanded Seylin, considerably startled. His King fixed him with a stern glance.

"Don't be a coward, boy! Your kingdom needs you," he admonished. "You'll strengthen the high families for generations."

"When you told me to see you about new employment," said Seylin bitterly, "I had no idea it would be fatherhood."

"Don't be silly," Marak laughed. "Fatherhood is just a hobby. No, I want you to become Catspaw's tutor. You and M will move to the tutor's quarters, on the floor below the royal rooms."

Seylin stared at him in complete amazement.

"You want me to tutor the new King?" he breathed. "But—I'm not too young for that?"

"Tutoring a King takes the better part of thirty years," observed Marak. "You won't be that young when you finish."

"King's magic!" exulted Seylin, his dark eyes shining. "Of course, I'll have to practice it before I teach it."

"Yes, the tutor has a workroom, too," said the King. "But you can't neglect the other subjects: elvish, dwarvish, English, history, strategy, economy, mathematics. I'll help, of course, but I can't do more than oversee and guide you."

"A King! What a pupil!" gloated Seylin. "He'll be able to learn anything!"

"He'll be able to learn anything and do it even better than you do," said Marak with a smile. "Catspaw's not quite six, but his magic is already much stronger than yours."

~

That afternoon, Tinsel slept soundly inside his indoor tent, but Sable roamed the large apartment in a state of near-panic. Her quarters had no balcony or terrace, a precaution against an important elf bride's attempting to throw herself to her death, and Tinsel had locked the door with magic so that she couldn't wander off while he slept. Sable had never been locked inside anything before. She found it completely unnerving. Even though her elf senses told her it was day outside, she paced her luxurious quarters like a caged animal, unable to sleep.

She wanted to get a drink and wash her face and hands, and she stood for several minutes in front of the shallow basin in her dressing room, unsure about what to do. Tinsel had shown her how the shiny metal knob made water gush out, but Sable was afraid of that fast-flowing water. Even if she had enough power to deal with it, she hadn't had a single magic lesson yet. What if she was able to start the water but not stop it? Perhaps the cave would flood. So she went back up the pathway and washed her face in the ornamental pool instead, while all the silver fish huddled in the shadows of their stone lily-pads.

A thumping noise startled her, and she scrambled to her feet. Someone was banging nearby. Sable crept noiselessly to the locked door of the apartment and found that the thumping came from it. She wished with all her heart that Tinsel were there with her, but he was still sleeping, and she was afraid to wake him up.

"Hello?" said a woman's voice through the door. It wasn't Irina's voice or Emily's. Sable breathed very quietly.

"Sable, are you there?" the voice continued. "I'm the goblin King's Wife. May I come in?"

The goblin King's Wife. She was the other elf. "I—yes—I don't know," stammered Sable. "I can't open the door."

"I can open it," answered the voice. "Is that all right? Are you dressed?"

"I think so," said Sable. She was wearing a long robe. Tinsel had thrown her rags away that morning.

The door opened, and a blond woman stood in the doorway, an elf Sable had never seen. She gave Sable a bright smile, and Sable managed a little smile back. Then a boy stepped past her, a goblin boy. She stared at him with wide eyes.

"May we come in?" asked the elf, and Sable backed up. She looked past the boy and gave a gasp. A large, hairy gray dog stood in the doorway.

"It's all right," the elf woman reassured her, and she turned to the big animal. "Helen, you'd better stay out in the hall." The dog put back her ears and wagged ingratiatingly.

"No, she can come, too," said Sable bravely, backing up farther and looking at the crowd that assembled in her apartment. The dog sat down, panting. The strange boy walked right up to Sable. He had short hair of two colors, dark blond and pale beige, the colors mixing in patches and streaks all over his head. He was watching her keenly with one blue eye and one green eye. She found it hard to look at him, but then she found it hard to look away.

"This is my son, Catspaw," said the elf woman, and Sable realized quite suddenly that the goblin boy did have a paw.

"I'm going to be the goblin King," announced the boy, planting himself before her and rocking back and forth from his heels to his toes. He waited for Sable to say something appreciative, but she didn't. "You're scared of me," he went on, watching her critically. "Why are you scared of me?"

"Catspaw," explained the woman, "Sable's only just come here, and she's been taught to be afraid of goblins. You'll have to show her that the goblin King's son can be a gentleman." The monster boy pondered this instruction for a few seconds, wearing a thoughtful frown. "And my name is Kate," continued the elf, smiling at Sable again. Sable glanced down, startled, as her hand was clasped. She hadn't been taught to shake hands.

"Is she a goblin, too?" she inquired timidly, pointing. Kate turned and looked. Helen gave a thump of her tail.

"Oh! No, she's just a dog," said Kate.

"Could be a goblin, though," declared the young prince suppor-tively. "See?"

There was a bright shimmer, and a half-grown wolf whelp stood on four feet where the boy had been. Three of the puppy's feet were gray, but the right front foot was still a golden lion's paw. A sec-ond shimmer, and the boy was back. Kate eyed Sable's shocked face with unease.

"Catspaw, you're not to do transformations unless Father's here," she reminded him firmly. "Why don't you have a seat and play with your mirror instead." The boy obediently sat down on the mat beside the fish pool, and Kate turned back to Sable.

"Did the dresses not fit?" she asked.

"Dresses? I don't have one," Sable replied distractedly. "Tinsel did something with mine, and I can't find it."

Kate looked at the black-haired woman. She considered all the horrible things Marak had told her, and she noted the lost, frightened look in those dark blue eyes.

"Come with me," she said kindly, taking Sable's hand, and she led the elf to the dressing room. Once there, she began pulling on knobs. The astonished Sable saw panels in the wall swing open and slide out to reveal all sorts of hidden cubbyholes.

Kate stepped confidently to the basin and brought warm water gushing into it. Then she taught Sable how to wash her face with soap and a cloth, how to clean her teeth, and how to trim her nails. She sat her down before the mirror and brushed out that long hair with a hairbrush, and she showed her how to pull it back with hair combs. She went to the drawers and closets and dressed the bemused elf woman in one undergarment after another, stockings, and slippers. Over it all went a long blue dress of some thin, shiny cloth, and then Kate stepped back to admire her work.

Sable stared at her reflection in the long mirror. She hardly recognized the beautiful woman who looked gravely back at her. This woman belonged in the elves' stories of ladies and queens, not in Sable's own life of deprivation and slavery. Only the wary eyes were the same. She still recognized them from before, and she ran her finger along the thin, faint lines that remained from her ghastly scars. She met Kate's approving gaze in the mirror and blushed.

"Two days ago, I was ugly," she said.

They went back to the ornamental pool, and Sable gave a squeak of fright. The goblin boy was watching a huge ant crawl around on the surface of his mirror.

"Catspaw, why don't you picture something nice," suggested Kate hurriedly.

"Ants are nice," protested the boy, but the ant disappeared. He caught sight of Sable in her new clothes and stood up. "You're pretty," he said, and he put his arms around her waist and looked up at her. "When I'm the goblin King, I'm going to marry an elf like Father did. I'm going to steal an elf bride just like you."

Kate, glancing at Sable's apprehensive expression, decided that this wasn't what she needed to hear.

"Well, you'll have to find one first, dear," she remarked briskly.

"I will," he promised, towing Sable over to sit by him at the ornamental pool. She watched him play with his magical mirror. Then she looked at Kate.

"And he's really your son," she said hesitantly. "I mean, he was your own baby."

"Oh, yes," laughed Kate. "He was my own baby."

Sable looked from one to the other of them. "I'm sorry," she said a little timidly. "I've never seen a mother and her baby before."

The smile left Kate's face.

"I know," she said. "Marak told me. It sounded so horrible." And her eyes filled with tears. Catspaw glanced up and saw them, and in another second he was in her lap.

"Mother, Mother, look," he said anxiously, holding up his mirror. "Look, Mother, I've made you a rose."

Irina and Sable began to find their place in the goblin kingdom, and if their comrades looked rather odd, at least their life was much more comfortable. Their new duties were more interesting, too because they had lessons in magic, elvish, and goblin, though the classes did give Irina quite a few difficult moments. Kate and Sable quickly formed a strong friendship, in spite of the fact that the two women came from such different worlds. They also had very different interests, as Kate was astonished to discover.

"What's this?" she asked one day, picking up some papers that Sable had brought to their elvish class. Sable glanced over and blushed.

"Tinsel's been showing me how math works," she admitted shyly. "I like to try problems when I have a few minutes alone. Numbers are so beautiful."

"Are they?" asked Kate in surprise, looking at the long-division problems. The goblins had never developed their own mathematics; instead because of their regular commerce with humans, they studied human mathematics. "I had to learn this, too," declared the blond woman, "but I thought language was much more beautiful."

"Oh, no," insisted Sable. "Numbers have such regular features. Languages are all lopsided and irregular, like goblins. If I know the word for 'dog,' I don't know the word for 'horse,' but if I know three and four, I know thirty, forty, three hundred, four hundred. And if I know three multiplied by three, I know three multiplied by thirty, and then division, which is multiplication in reverse. All the patterns are so beautiful, and they always come true. Numbers are something you can depend on."

Kate pondered this. It had never occurred to her that someone might like numbers more than words. She told Marak about it, and he found it equally interesting. Before their next magic lesson, he handed Sable a piece of paper.

"What's this?" she asked cautiously, looking at the complicated figures drawn on it. She still found the proximity of the goblin King unnerving.

"It's a new class just for you," he answered. "I'm going to teach you elvish mathematics."

Sable brightened, attracted by the thought of the math. "But I can't read this," she pointed out.

"No, you can't," he agreed. "The elves didn't use human numbers for their math. They developed their own."

"What did they use their math for?" asked Sable.

"Use?" Marak chuckled. "They didn't use it at all. They played with it, just like they did with everything. Elves liked to study geometric figures, but not like the ones you may have learned from Tinsel. Their geometry is in motion: a planet forming different figures as it crosses a constellation, or a dance of two circles, one going one way and one going the other, with dancers weaving in and out between them. The elves developed their math to describe all those moving figures, as if anyone would ever want to do that."

Sable was fascinated at the thought of those complex patterns.

"How do you know all this?" she asked.

"I wasted three years of my life studying elvish mathematics," he said. "My son will, too, and the pages learn a smattering of it as well. It exercises the mind, and that's about all. It's not anything I've used once I learned it. Sometimes, when I'm falling asleep, the beautiful figures from elvish math will drift around in my head. Poor elves, that's all they gave the world, a few pretty dreams."

If elvish math was useless and beautiful, it also turned out to be very hard. One problem could take all afternoon. Marak was impressed by Sable's rapid progress and pleased with her powerful interest in it. "So elvish math has a use after all," he commented to Kate.

Marak taught the three elf women magic twice a week. Kate and Sable were strong rivals in class, but Irina was perfectly content to stay in last place.

One day, he put an odd handful of ingredients in front of each of them. Kate studied her handful. It looked like a combination of uncarded wool, plant stems, seeds, and crumbled leaves.

"Starting today, you're going to learn how elf clothing is made," announced the King. "Most of these ingredients are common forest plants. The elves took their wool from their own flocks of sheep, which ran loose in the elf King's forest. Once a year, the elves called in the sheep and worked the Shearing Spell, peeling the wool right off. The protection spells on the sheep were renewed, and the sheep were free once more. You can see," he added dryly, "that the elves' life didn't involve much hard work."

"Mine did," sighed Irina, and Marak patted her on the shoulder as he walked to his own pile of ingredients.

"What you see before you is the raw material of elf yarn," he told

them. "The spell for making yarn centers on the Harp constellation." He pointed to it on the star chart. "The First Fathers of the
elves noticed how much a loom looks like a harp, so the spells for
clothing are full of musical ideas. To make yarn, you cup your hand
loosely over the ingredients before you, find the Harp in your mind,
and recite the following phrase, '*gutesha-si shir,*' which means 'voices
blending in a single melody.'" Marak looked at his ingredients,
frowning in concentration. "And then," he said, cupping his hand
over the pile, "with your other hand——"

"You do this."

Marak looked up. Irina was pulling fine brown yarn out from
under her cupped hand, just as steadily and easily as if she were hiding a spool beneath her fingers.

"Yes, that's what you do," murmured Marak, watching her.
"Kate and Sable, you try now."

After a few false starts, Sable got a sort of string going, but it kept
getting fatter and thinner. Kate produced crumbled leaves stuck
together in a long line, and Sable's string tangled and broke off.

"Keep trying," said their teacher. "It's not an easy spell." The
two women looked at each other and then at Irina. A fist-sized pile
of perfect yarn lay by her rapidly moving fingers.

"Marak, I need more of that stuff," Irina announced happily.
"I've run out."

Kate had never found a magic class so long before. After quite a
bit of work, Sable could produce a rough yarn, but Kate's efforts
continually frizzed or clumped back into plant bits.

"You'll notice that we've been working on brown yarn, for winter
clothes," remarked their teacher. "In order to make green yarn, you
add *nisakha,* 'of spring,' to the end of your spell, making it 'voices
blending in a single melody of spring.' I'd like you to try making green
yarn for next time. Kate, why don't you stay for a few minutes. I'll help
you practice."

By next class, Sable had a tolerable brown yarn to exhibit, but her green yarn was more of a brown-green tweed. Kate shamefacedly exhibited a handful of rough twine. It was dark gray, speckled all over with pale wool fibers.

"Did you make green yarn?" Marak asked Irina with interest.

"Oh, yes," she answered readily, reaching into her bag. "First I made green for a while," and she pulled out a neat skein of beautiful, soft green yarn. "Then I went back to brown again," and she pulled out another skein, of lovely brown yarn. "But then I got tired of green and brown," she confessed. "They're so boring. I started to play with the spell, and first I made black because that's a melody of the night, you know," and she pulled out a handful of jet black yarn. "And then I made red because that's a melody of the heart."

Marak picked up the skeins and studied them carefully.

"That's wonderful, Irina," he remarked. "I've never read of any elf using the spell this way before." At the end of class, he asked them to continue working on their brown and green yarn. "But, Irina," he said, "I'd like you to see how many different colors you can make."

For the next three days, Irina could be seen at work on her yarn, sitting in the hall staring at a particular mosaic tile or looking out the window at the deep blue color of the lake valley sky. When class came again, she had fifty-six different colors to exhibit, including a bright, metallic yarn that she had modeled on Tinsel's hair.

Marak showed them how to make their yarn into cloth, a process more like knitting than weaving, so it produced a stretchy fabric. He assigned them to try it for homework. Sable had a modest swatch of green cloth to exhibit on the appointed day. Kate produced something that looked like a rag for scrubbing dishes, and her eyes dared the goblin King to comment. He didn't, of course, but he was aware of its history. He privately felt that it would have turned out better if she hadn't flung it against the wall so many times.

When called upon to exhibit her cloth, Irina pulled out a beautiful tunic of blended green and blue yarn.

"This is for the prince," she explained. "I got the idea because his eyes are green and blue. I used two yarns at the same time as I worked the spell, and that makes the whole thing so much more interesting because sometimes you look at it and see the green and sometimes the blue."

"But, Irina," said the goblin King, stunned, "I haven't taught you how to make the cloth into clothing yet. I haven't taught you how to join the seams." Irina's tunic had perfect elf seams, which is to say, no seams were there at all. The garment appeared to have been made all in one piece.

"Sure, you taught me," said Irina carelessly, and when he shook his head, she giggled. "You're always joking," she observed.

"Marak," asked Kate plaintively that evening, untangling her elf cloth, which kept knitting itself into a ball, "if Irina's so bad at magic, how can she be so good at this?"

"Most magical people have a special talent," he replied from the checkers game he and Catspaw were playing. "Almost all of Irina's magic is concentrated in this one talent. She has an astounding gift for textiles. Other elf women doubtless had it, too, but because of their upbringing, it never would have occurred to them to make cloth that wasn't green or brown. Irina's mind is open to new ideas, so she's trying all sorts of things. I can't wait to see her final project."

Marak had asked them to make any item of cloth or clothing they would like as their final project. Kate glanced down unhappily. She was making a scarf. It was useless in the goblin kingdom, but it was the easiest thing she knew.

"I'm supposed to have all this magic," she said with a frown, "and Sable outdoes me about half the time."

"It's a shame I can't teach you defense magic," murmured the goblin King. "Your attack and dismemberment spells would astound the class." He made a motion with his hand, and his checker jumped one of Catspaw's checkers. Then it seized the unlucky checker and ate it.

"I don't want to dismember anyone!" exclaimed Kate in horror.

"You just think you don't," remarked her husband absently. "But I'll bet you enjoyed beheading the sorcerer." Catspaw's checker jumped one of his. Then it jumped up and down on his checker until it was tiny bits.

Kate thought about that, smoothing out her snarled brown cloth. Almost seven years before, when her husband and half the King's Guard had been enslaved by a human sorcerer, she had left the kingdom to rescue them, and while that sorcerer lay before her, helpless and paralyzed, she had beheaded him with one blow of a sword. She enjoyed thinking about how she had saved her little girl, Til, from that horrible man, and she enjoyed thinking about liberating the goblins. But she never, ever let herself think about the satisfaction she had felt when she saw the sorcerer's head roll across the floor. Ladies didn't enjoy doing such things. She felt supremely annoyed at Marak for bringing it up.

"What's your special talent?" she demanded. "You never have a problem with any magic."

"That's different," chuckled Marak. "I'm a King. I have as much magic as about twenty of you, maybe more. Besides, not all magic is as easy for me as you think. I really have to concentrate on my dwarf spells."

"I'm so sorry for you," said Kate bitterly. Her elf cloth rolled up and fused itself into a solid mass. Marak waved his hand, and one of his checkers reached the last row. It blossomed into a golden crown and did a small victory jig.

Class time came again, and Kate produced her brown scarf. It looked as if it had already been worn for several years, perhaps by a cart horse.

"Very good," said the goblin King.

"Don't start," warned his wife.

Sable produced a tunic and breeches that she had made for Tinsel. She had spent a humbling afternoon with Irina learning how to make black cloth and getting help on the seams.

"Beautiful!" commented Marak. "Nice, even color, very well made. He has my permission to wear this on duty."

Sable glowed with pleasure. "But he doesn't have to," she protested modestly. "I like Tinsel in black anyway. It goes with his coloring."

They turned to Irina. She had been very secretive about her project, and not even Sable had managed to pry loose a clue. Now she reached into her bag and unrolled a tapestry about three feet square.

"This is the lake where we had our summer camp," she explained to her dumbfounded audience. "It was always my favorite camp. I was born there. You see this little grove of birches here, but most of it is oak and ash. The full moon shows up twice because it's high enough to shine in the water, and I never really saw a stag on the hill like that, but I put him in because deer are just so pretty, don't you think?"

"This is an amazing achievement," said Marak, putting his arm around her. "After lunch, I'd like to introduce you to two of our best weavers. You'll think they look funny, but they're very nice, and they're the strongest elf-cross weavers I have. I hope that you'll agree to work with them."

"Oh, good," said the elf girl, beaming up at him. "Are they going to teach me how to weave?"

"No, Irina," said the goblin King thoughtfully. "I'm hoping that you can teach them."

Chapter Sixteen

As the months passed, all three of the marriages that came from the elf quest prospered. Marak was satisfied that the elf women were happy, and he wasn't surprised that his own wife was happier, too. Kate had found a real friend in Sable. The two women spent lots of time together, studying their lessons or just talking about life.

Sable did have a moderate talent for healing, but she didn't pursue it. The suffering she had been through made her nervous and unhappy around those who were in pain, and it soon became apparent that her heart and a large share of her magic belonged to mathematics. Poring over the old texts in the King's library, she mastered all that was known of elvish math and went on to develop it in ways that no goblin had ever considered.

Always ready to exploit a resource, Marak asked Sable to work with the dwarves on their building and decorating projects. Ordinarily, these two races had nothing to offer each other: the dwarves suffered from a kind of reverse claustrophobia if removed from their mines and tunnels, and the captive elves of past days had always longed for the outside world and the sky. But Sable's interest in mathematical patterns matched the taste of the dwarves who had a talent for architecture. Together, they renovated some of the palace's most important spaces.

Irina caused a sensation in the goblin world. Without a doubt, she was the most imaginative elvish dress designer who had ever lived, and her bold use of color and texture made her a celebrity among the fashion-conscious goblins. Impossible to imitate, difficult to obtain, an original Irina gown was the finishing touch to any special occasion. But money and prestige were not enough to secure one. Irina's clients soon learned that the amiable elf woman enjoyed company. Those who stopped by her busy workroom found their projects moved to the head of the list. Thus the awkward, unwanted tag-along girl from the elf camp days soon found herself in the center of an adoring throng.

Only one person in the kingdom disliked the newcomers from the very start, and nothing could change her mind. Kate's human foster daughter Til had been the leader of an exclusive clique among the pages, but Richard's coming had wrecked it. The foundling who knew how to pick pockets and survive in the daylight world seemed to be everyone's darling. He could tell stories about scary human criminals and smoky London alleys, and he mesmerized the impressionable pages. Richard rapidly developed into a favorite in the guardroom as well. With his streetwise smarts and easy, likable nature, he was equally at home in a gathering of grownups or children. People stopped taking notice of the infuriated Til.

Even worse, Til felt that she was losing her hold on Kate, whom she had always viewed as her special property. From the day Til had arrived in the kingdom as a baby, the little girl whom Kate had found in the sorcerer's lair had been the center of Kate's world. Catspaw's birth hadn't done much to change this. Kate loved her son, but she didn't understand his goblin nature that well, and he was even-tempered and independent. Til, on the other hand, fought hard to get as much attention as she could. With Kate, she usually succeeded.

Now Kate had new friends and interests, and she didn't dote on the child anymore. Til's life among the pages took her away from her foster mother for days at a time, and Kate no longer pined for her little girl. In fact, as Til aged and her temper became increasingly tempestuous, Kate found herself more and more distressed by her daughter's behavior. The reserved woman couldn't identify with Til's vanity and ambition. When her attempts to manage the head strong girl failed, Kate began to find excuses to spend less time with her.

In doing this, the King's Wife was merely behaving like an elf, as Marak noted to the interested Seylin. "She did the same thing when M was growing up," he remarked. "She can't fight her nature. Elves don't tolerate negative emotion well at all. If someone's behavior becomes too upsetting, an elf simply stops speaking to him." This analysis was undoubtedly true, but Kate's reticence did Til little good, and the girl's conduct grew worse and worse.

There were many things that Til despised, but as the years passed, Catspaw came to top them all. It wasn't that the goblin prince was particularly cruel to her; he was usually completely indif ferent. The stormy closeness of their early childhood was only a dis tant memory. Til moved in one circle of peers, and Catspaw in another. Even in boyhood, he was gaining magical power, confi dence, and prestige. Til's younger sibling, respected by all, was being groomed to take over his kingdom. His ambitious foster sister felt that this was completely unfair.

The prince was shaping up to be a particularly promising ruler. From Kate, whose elvish roots almost certainly went back to the elf King's lieutenants, Catspaw had inherited a stunning amount of military magic, and with it came a real enthusiasm for the art of war. The young prince gathered about himself boys from the high fami lies to join him in goblin games of strategy and battle. Richard, gifted as well with military magic, became his favorite opponent.

One day, when Til was close to fourteen years old, she came up the stairs to her parents' floor to complain to them about some imag ined offense. But she couldn't even reach their rooms. Catspaw and Richard had taken over the broad hallway for their war games and had temporarily altered it past recognition. Instead of polished gold, the hall floor had erupted into miniature mountains, hills, valleys, and canyons. Over these, like ants, marched the phantom troops of the two warriors, who studied their ground and laid their plans. Behind the last mountain range, and before the doors that were her goal, the goblin guards watched the sport and made quiet wagers.

"Get this junk out of the way!" she demanded, walking up behind Catspaw. "I have to see Papa."

Her foster brother was too busy to respond. He was in the middle of an assault against the vanguard of Richard's army. The minuscule cavalry at his feet wheeled and charged, uttering faint war cries.

"Marak isn't at home," one guard related. "He's out inspecting the harvest, and the King's Wife has gone for a walk."

The thwarted girl seethed with irritation. She aimed a kick at a marching column of Catspaw's reinforcements, causing terrible slaughter. Tiny soldiers dragged their injured comrades out of danger. A chorus of quiet groans arose, like a regretful sigh.

Catspaw knelt to resuscitate his fallen forces, irritated in his turn. "Til, no one wants you here," he declared. "Go back to the pages' floor."

Til felt both the truth and the injustice of this remark and drew herself up to her full height. She might not be magical royalty, but she was half a head taller than he was.

"I'll do what I like! I'll never do what you say," she declaimed dramatically. She noted with displeasure that the guards exchanged amused glances, and Richard looked up and grinned.

"Of course you will," remarked Catspaw. "When I'm the King, you'll have to."

The veracity of this statement only infuriated the girl more. She struck out as best she could. "You're going to be a terrible King," she announced coldly. "Everyone knows it. They just don't tell you."

Catspaw's magic detected the lie at once. It didn't bother the boy that there were witnesses to the insult. He lived his entire life out in public. Schooled by Kate to be a gentleman, he glanced over his shoulder and gave Til a condescending smile.

"I wouldn't dream of contradicting you," he said and turned back to his battlefield.

Til went on the attack again, but this time with more cunning. Combat of a social sort was her own special forte; she gained her greatest satisfaction from the embarrassment and discomfort of others. She knew the prince's abilities, and she was also aware of his limitations. She worked out a battle plan of her own.

"Mama cried when she first saw you," she remarked.

"I know she did," responded Catspaw casually. "Seylin says that's normal when an elf bride sees her baby."

"She didn't cry because she was seeing any old goblin," continued Til carefully. "She cried because of you. I heard her talking to Sable one day. She said she knows that you'll never be a man like your father."

The prince's magic found no lie in these statements because each one was perfectly true. Together, they formed a lie, but his magic couldn't discern this. It didn't occur to Catspaw that Kate might be pleased to have raised a son different in many ways from her husband. The prince had two serious weaknesses: his loving regard for his mother and his unspoken awe of his father. The goblin King cast a very long shadow over the boy, a shadow from which he might never be great enough to emerge. If Til had spent years trying to think up ways to hurt him, she couldn't have found a better plan.

The goblin prince turned to face his foster sister. Dead pale, eyes blazing, he held out his lion's paw. A gust of wind swept across the landing and caught up the triumphant Til. She spun around in it, coming to rest against the wall, where she flattened out like a sheet of paper. In an instant, she was trapped in two inflexible dimensions.

A full-length mirror hung on the wall now, with the struggling girl pinned inside.

"I can't move! I can't breathe!" cried the desperate Til. She tried to turn her head, to move her arms, but there was nowhere to go. She had nothing but height, width, and a voice that was growing more frantic by the second.

"'To hold, as 'twere, the mirror up to nature,'" declared the boy from the depths of his fury. "That's you—all surface. Nothing behind the show." The mirror fell forward and hit the floor with a splintering crash. "Too bad, Til," he added remorselessly. "Seven years of bad luck."

Seylin heard the sonorous explosion and ensuing shrieks and ran up the stairs two at a time. He found Til sitting by the wall, her face and hands criss-crossed by a net of red lines. He knelt down beside the hysterical girl and discovered that they were shallow cuts oozing blood.

"What happened?" he asked Catspaw. His pupil's expression was distant.

"She shattered," the boy calmly replied. "It's only an illusion." A second later, the bleeding lines were gone, but Til still sobbed with fear and rage. Seylin tried to put a comforting arm around her, but she shoved him away.

"I'm surprised at you, Catspaw!" said the tutor, and his face showed his dismay. "You're too old and far too powerful to be giving way to your temper! A king has to use his abilities to help and protect the weak. Apologize to Til at once."

Catspaw turned to the weeping girl.

"I'm very sorry, Til, that you're so weak and I'm so strong," he told her in a steady voice. "I wish we could fight as equals. If you have any sense, you'll stay away from me. I'm not an enemy you can handle."

Til gathered herself up with a glare at them all and went off down the stairs. Nonplussed, Seylin stared after her. He stood up and turned to confront his pupil, but what he saw astonished him further. There was a look of decision, of authority, on the boy's face that he had never seen there before.

"I will protect the weak," declared the prince coldly. "But that doesn't include my enemies. I'll deal with them as I decide, and it's going to be too bad for them if they're weak."

Seylin understood what was happening. The prince's childhood was ending. Before, Catspaw had always obeyed him simply because it was expected. He would doubtless continue to do so, but it would never again be automatic. It would be a magnanimous gesture from now on, a generous gift from a superior to his underling. And the day would come when his royal pupil wouldn't obey him at all. Instead, Seylin noted with rueful unease, he himself would be the one who would obey.

Catspaw was becoming a real goblin King.